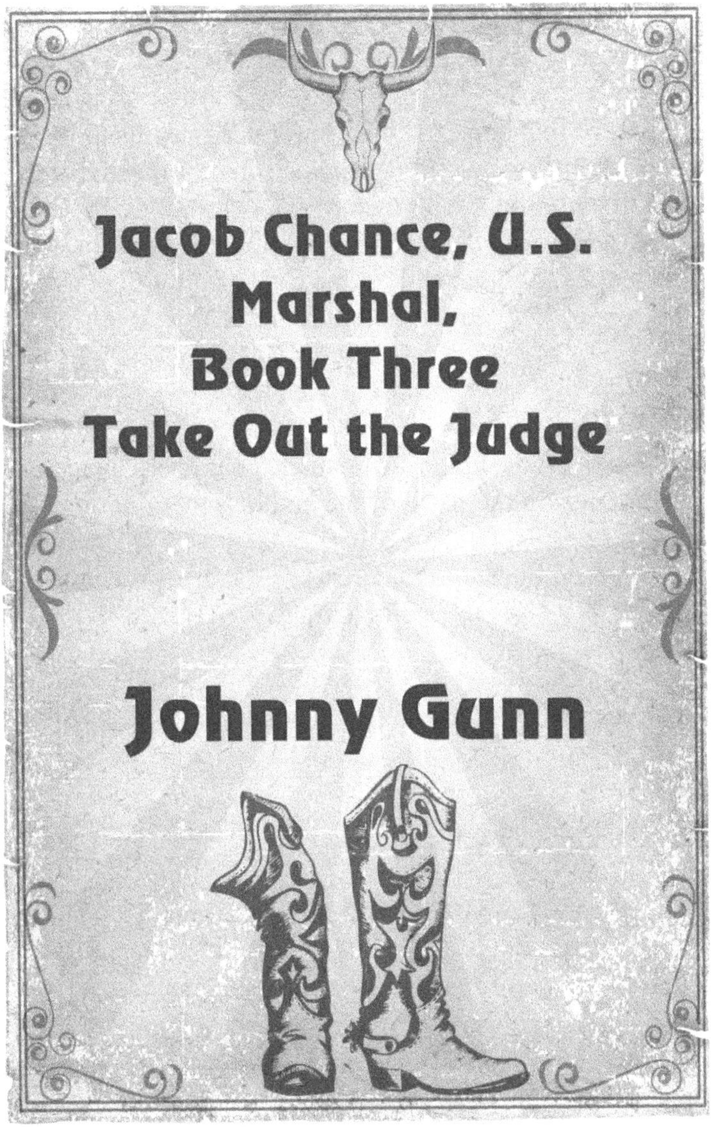

Jacob Chance, U.S. Marshal, Book Three Take Out the Judge

Johnny Gunn

Solstice Publishing - www.solsticepublishing.com

Take Out the Judge

A Jacob Chance Novel

By Johnny Gunn

Dedication

To my lovely bride, Patty. I could never do this without her backing me up.

Chapter One

"It's not that hard to understand, Spencer. You see to it that judge finds in our favor or I open the door to Spade Dooley. You've got two weeks, and I want that judgment in before then." Nate Burleson was a large, intimidating man who demanded that he get his way, or else. If it meant killing a judge to get his way, so be it. "If that court nullifies the current water law, it will be difficult if not impossible for the legislature to resurrect it."

Spade Dooley ran a gang of killers, card sharks, and ne'er-do-wells, and was feared by many in western Nevada. His guns, knives, and men were available for hire, if they weren't on a job of their own first.

"Stanfield is a hard man to deal with, Burleson," Harold Spencer said. "All I can do is give it my best." Spencer was a slimy attorney who worked for a group of large ranchers in the area. These men were rich, arrogant, and selfish, and Spencer's job was to do their bidding, and make it seem that it was being done within the letter of the law.

"It better be what I just said," Nathaniel Burleson answered back. The meeting was taking place in the offices of Harold Spencer, attorney, just two blocks from the Nevada State Capitol building in Carson City. Nathaniel Burleson was a large landholder in the Carson Valley, determined that water on his property was his and his alone. Sitting at the table was mine owner August Kastner, who too believed that whatever water was on a property belonged to that property, no matter the size or origin of that water.

Nevada came about because of an immense silver strike just fifteen miles to the north known as the Comstock

Mining District, and the town of Virginia City now sits on top of those incredibly rich mines. Along with gold and silver, in that very dry state water was often as valuable, and more than one war had been fought over it.

The Nevada Legislature had been battling water rights questions for two sessions and had not delivered a set of laws to cover the questions. The old territorial laws simply didn't answer the questions that had been raised. With statehood, population growth, and federal intervention, the questions were boiling over into threatened violence. More than one property owner had been shot trying to protect or take water. More than one mine had hired muscle to enact their own water rights rules. And there was no law on the books for anyone to fall back on.

There were vast areas of the new Silver State where people were establishing ranches and taking property without following the few property laws that existed, and those people didn't want to be told by some so-called Supreme Court justice that they didn't have a right to the water or the land they called their own.

Nevada Supreme Court Justice Amos Stanfield was in the process of writing a court document on the issue, following a favorable ruling by the body, and the question had become heated to the point that ranchers like Burleson were looking to hire guns to settle the issue. Spade Dooley, known throughout the Silver State and surrounding states as a vicious killer, bank robber, and gang leader had been approached by Burleson and Kastner, and was ready to assassinate Stanfield at a moment's notice, if he didn't come down on their side.

There was a timetable that was held as a hammer over both sides. The legislature was scheduled to begin their next session on or about February 1, Stanfield had promised his opinion would be issued prior to that, and February 1 was just seven weeks away. "Now you listen to me, Spencer," Burleson stormed, "with Christmas, New Years, and a cold miserable winter, we are almost out of time. I want Stanfield in our pocket, guaranteed, or I take the chains from Dooley." He glared at the attorney, chewed his cigar like a tough piece of range bull, and marched from the office.

***

Stanfield was having a late breakfast at the St. Charles Hotel, doing his best to answer questions from a young hotshot reporter named Mark Twain, down from his perch at the *Territorial Enterprise* in Virginia City. "Now, Mark, this is your second legislative session and you know what the water questions are. That's why my opinion has to answer every question, and be consistent. There's no doubt the ranchers, farmers, and miners have rights to the state's water, but so does the rest of the populace."

"Well, now, see here, Amos, that's just it. Does the state own the water, and if so, why? And, why would Mr. Citizen have a right to any water other than his own well?" Twain had been on a first name basis with the state's leaders almost from his first day in Nevada. His brother, Orion Clemens, had been appointed Territorial Secretary and brought his younger brother along as his secretary. Twain gave that up, tried mining, and found his life's blood in writing.

After some serious political fighting, Carson City became the capital, but Virginia City was the largest city in the new state and swung some heavy political weight when it felt the need. The *Territorial Enterprise* was the leading news journal in the state.

"I don't think there are easy answers to any of those questions, my young friend," Stanfield said. "The thing is, if you have water running through your property, say as the Carson River runs through the valley, can you simply take every drop you want, or should you only be allowed to have so much? And, why? I don't think a rancher should be able to take more than what would be needed.

"That's our debate, Mr. Twain, sir, and it's the allocation of that water that needs to be specifically written into law, with enough breathing room for all entities to be able to live with the law."

Twain finished his snifter of good Kentucky bourbon, shook hands with the jurist, and smiled just a bit. "Glad all I have to do is write a few words that won't make any sense and nobody will remember tomorrow," he said. "Your words strike like lightning and last forever."

The weight of those words was the cause of the frown that Stanfield wore when he returned to his offices and found Harold Spencer once again waiting for him. "Spencer, if you continue this constant pestering I'm going to file harassment charges with the sheriff. I will not stand for this one more minute. Get out of my office now," and the old judge stormed to his desk, ripping a drawer open and coming up with an old gamblers single shot pistol.

Spencer beat a hasty retreat, offering a threat on his way out the door. "You'll regret this, Stanfield. My clients have friends, you know." Stanfield raised that little derringer and pulled the hammer back, and Spencer, his coattails flapping as he ran down the marble steps of the Supreme Court Building, had fear written across his face, expecting a bullet in his back.

Stanfield had the smirk of a winner spread across his face when he sat down at his desk. He looked at the old gun and smiled even more. *Doesn't even have a cap on the nipple*, he chuckled, but also recognized the threat that had been hurled. He penned a quick note to the state's attorney general, Elmer Barlow, outlining the threat and wondering if the state had plans to offer protection to its judiciary.

Stanfield had been a district judge before his appointment to Nevada's highest bench and had worked with local law enforcement many times. He was most fond of memories of working closely with members of the United States Marshal Service during a time of lawlessness in Preston, Nevada.

In his note to Barlow, Stanfield outlined how the Marshal Service was formed for the protection of the federal judiciary, and maybe the state should have something of the kind. His thoughts drifted off to those weeks he spent in Preston and his friendship with U.S. Marshals Jacob Chance and Ira Stone.

"Chance was the key with his strength and intellect, and Stone with his knowledge of the law, those poor bastards with their land fraud schemes didn't stand a chance." He chuckled. He could see Chance standing there in his serape and floppy sombrero, long and tall, and enjoyed the thought of Ira Stone always chomping on an unlit cigar.

That's what I need right now, he thought. *Chance and Stone riding herd on that fool attorney Spencer. Threaten me, you slimy little bastard, and I'll sic the marshals on your skinny butt.*

Chapter Two

"I'm not having any luck on slowing Papa down about a big Christmas party again, Jacob. You just have to talk to him." Jennifer Chance walked into the large barn on their ranch, some twenty-five miles north of Preston, Nevada. It was winter in the Golden Valley, cold and windy, but very little snow so far this season. Jennifer's father, Ben Stokes, was one of the original ranchers in the Golden Valley.

When he retired, he sold his ranch to Jacob and Jennifer, and they combined it with their homestead, giving Ben the old ranch house to live in for the rest of his life. He had had a passion for big parties all his life, and the community Christmas bar-b-q was always the biggest and, generally, the most fun. Winter weather was not a deterrent.

"When I told him it's out of the question he just laughed and said you didn't think so. Are you in cahoots with him?" Ben Stokes had been hosting large Christmas parties at his ranch for so many years that many in the valley just assumed the tradition would continue forever.

"You know how much Christmas means to that man, Jenny," Jacob Chance said, stepping out of one of the stalls lining the west wall of the barn. He was leading a colt that was high-stepping alongside. "Just look at this pretty little boy, Jenny. This is Mr. Morgan's progeny, and I might just keep him for myself."

Jacob Chance had been riding his black Morgan stud for many years, and with his breeding program at the ranch, was using the horse to breed many of the mares he had imported from California, from Mexican and Spanish stock dating back to the 1600s.

"We really do have to talk about this, Jacob. Papa is too old to be trying to put on another huge Christmas party." They walked out of the barn toward one of the round pens where Jacob and his Mexican horse boss, Juan Ortega, worked their stock horses. Jacob turned the young one loose in the pen and slipped his arms around Jennifer.

"For your information, lovely wife of mine, Ben Stokes has a co-conspirator in this plan you're arguing against. Actually, three co-conspirators, and you, dear lady, are outnumbered and outvoted. We'll have that party at Ben's house just as we have had each year since we've been married."

"What do you mean three co-conspirators?" she asked, stepping back to look him straight in the eye.

"Well," the tall, lanky cowboy in a floppy sombrero and rugged bearskin coat said with a boyish grin, "there would be me, Jacob Chance," and he paused just a bit, "there would be little Jake, your first-born," and another pause, "and there would be little Missy, one Sarah Jean Chance, your youngest child."

"All of you have been planning this with Papa?"

"Yup," is all Chance said, sweeping Jennifer into his strong arms and planting a big wet kiss on her lips, taking the opportunity to gently give her little bottom a nice pat or two. They walked toward the back door of the big ranch house for a late morning cup of coffee. "Besides, Ben Stokes ain't anywhere near being an old man. He just wants to be so he doesn't have to do much work," he chuckled.

She gave him a good swat when he opened the kitchen door for her. "It's not fair for you all to gang up on me like that." She snickered, heading for the big cook stove and a boiling pot of coffee. "I suppose you've even sent out invitations?" She pouted, but with a smile she was trying to suppress.

"We need to talk about something that's a bunch more important, Jenny," Chance said, taking a seat at their large kitchen table. "We had that big fight over land and water fraud eight years ago, and the snake's head is bobbing at us again, this time by way of the state legislature. Jerrod Stockton wants me to come to Carson City in February to testify on the new land and water laws that'er being discussed.

"Seems that somebody has been offering large sums of money to many of the legislators to vote a certain way, and there were implied threats against them and their families if they didn't accept the bribe. Jerrod showed me a letter he got, and he said it appeared that many of those involved would take the bribes."

Jerrod Stockton was the blacksmith that fought side-by-side with Jacob Chance when the former U.S. marshal had been sent to Preston, then Nevada Territory, to challenge men who were stealing land, water, and the rights of ranchers in the Golden Valley.

The death and destruction from those times still burned in the minds of those that lived in Preston and the surrounding ranches. Because of the battles waged by Marshal Chance and the citizens of the area, a real community developed, and natural leadership came to the fore. Among those real leaders was the blacksmith Stockton.

When the actual town of Preston developed, Stockton was the first mayor, and he did such a fine job that he was elected to the Nevada State Senate, representing Esmeralda County. "It's getting pretty nasty in some sections of the state. Buck Colby and Juan Ortega can take care of this old ranch for a few weeks, and I think you and the children would enjoy visiting the capital city."

"That's a wonderful idea, Chance. Missy isn't old enough to understand what it would be all about, but what an education Jake would get. Yes, and you're putting this all together just so I'll go along with the big Christmas party, aren't you, you conniving critter. That's why I married you.

"But there's more to it, isn't there?"

He was laughing gently when he poured another cup of coffee and mentioned that Ira Stone had gotten married and would bring his new wife to the Christmas party. Stone served in the Marshal Service with Chance and when Stone retired, he was named U.S. attorney for the state of Nevada. "In his letter, he says that Rebecca is just as pretty as you are."

"It'll be so good to see him again, and I'm glad he's settled down," Jennifer said, and then swatted Chance one more time. "You were saving that little tidbit up in case I really got nasty about the Christmas party, weren't you. Oh, Chance, you are a sneaky one," she said, hearing the chortles across the table. "I guess, then, that you and Dad, the children and former marshals, have seen to it that, what, half of Carson City will descend on us?" She got up and brought the coffee pot to the table, pouring more of the boiling coffee in their cups.

"Yup, seems that way," he said, winking at her and giving a big smile. "Ira is doing what he can to convince Amos Stanfield to come, too, but he's in the middle of writing what might end up as Nevada's water law. I'm sure glad he's doing that, and not some of the hotheads I've heard about up north. If it weren't for Judge Stanfield, the Golden Valley would still be in a war over water and land rights. He was appointed to the state's Supreme Court, and he's writing the majority opinion in the case. Says it needs to be done before the legislature meets in February."

"I just saw a big black cloud wash across that rugged face of yours, Chance. What was that all about?"

"Ira said there have been threats made, and he's not sure the Capitol Police Department is up to the challenge."

"I smell something else, Chance," she said, feeling her body tighten up, getting that surge of protectiveness spreading through her system. "Exactly what did Ira say in that letter?"

"He wants me to ride back to Carson City with him as soon as the Christmas party is over. Ira Stone has more investigative sense than any ten marshals I worked with over the years, Jenny, and he is sure he sees a conspiracy developing between some of the Carson Valley ranchers and some of the mining interests in the state, and from what I've heard about Stanfield's written opinion coming up, his life may be in danger.

"Those people do not want that opinion written. They want the legislature to write the law, which is the way it should be, but many in the legislature have been intimidated by those ranching and mining interests. Or bought off, if you will."

"What can you do, Jacob Chance?" she said, knowing that he would once again ride into danger. "I don't want you to put that badge back on."

"No, I won't do that, Jenny. This is strictly a state matter, a threat to a state judge, but Stone wants me to talk to the judge and build a security net around him. He did so much for us here in Preston, Jenny," he said, almost pleading. "I feel a tremendous responsibility to Stanfield. If he needs protection, then I want to be the one to give it. You and the children can join me in Carson City when the legislature is in session in February."

"I don't know why I had to fall in love with a man who takes personal responsibility to such a high level." She smiled at him, reaching across the table for his hand. "Who else is behind this scheme to have a Christmas party? That's next week, you know. I'll have to spend every waking hour making bread and baking pies, Jacob Chance."

"Ben and I are gonna roast a young steer on the rotisserie, Cotton Phelps and Jerrod will bring ducks and geese to roast, and Hank Adams said he has a perfect lamb for the roasting pits. Ben has invited the whole town, it seems. Sarah Phelps said that she will help you with all the things that need to be done, and Eileen will also do anything you ask, she said."

"I'm glad Eileen and Jerrod got married. They are a sight to see." She laughed. "He's as big as a barn and she's just a pip-squeak. Well, Marshal Chance, sir, I'm sure glad you waited until now to let me in on this little enterprise you and my dad have put together. Any other surprises on this fine winter's day?"

"I think I hear Juan yelling at me." He smiled, getting up from the table. "I better get back out to the corrals." He chuckled all the way out the door, expecting to find a dish towel or maybe something heavier aimed at his head. He found his ranch foreman, Buck Colby, talking with Juan Ortega at the corrals.

"Got that feeder steer in the holding corral, boss," Colby said. "He'll be just right for roasting. We'll let him hang for four days, and we'll have to start cooking pretty early if we want to eat at midday. I have four men cutting oak, so we'll have some fine coals to cook that meat."

"Good, Buck, thanks," Chance said. "I'm glad the party's at Ben's and not here. I'm probably going to leave for Carson City right after the party, and I want you and Juan to make sure this ranch runs well, and I want you two to take special care of my family.

"They will be coming to the capital in February, probably the end of January, everything based on the weather, of course, and Buck, I want you and at least two of our men to escort them up. Missy is awfully young, Jake is a good hand, and it will be winter. You bring them to me safe."

"They'll be safe, well fed, and warm, Jacob, I promise," Colby said. "That's a long lonesome ride from here north. Even the stage line gets in trouble once in a while. We'll bring plenty of food and blankets, and I'll bring 'em in safe.

"While I've got your attention, I'm sure we're going to have a very large calf crop this year, Jacob. Those bulls you acquired got into their work, good. I've counted hundreds of pregnant heifers out there."

"That's good news, Buck. What do the mares look like, Juan?" Chance asked his horse boss.

"Only one mare didn't take, Jefe," Ortega answered. "We'll have some good foals later this spring. We talked about a spring sale of some of those two- and three-year-olds. You still planning on that? We could do a June sale and offer at least twenty or more colts and fillies."

"That'll give us plenty of time to work 'em, Juan. Pick a good date, and I'll spread the word when I'm in Carson City. Our horses have a pretty good reputation, thanks to you and your hard work."

***

"Amos, we've been friends ever since that ruckus in Preston several years ago, and you know how I feel about Jacob Chance. I'm positive there're threats being made as we speak and I want you protected. I want Chance to come to Carson City as soon as the Christmas festivities are over and set up a protection net around you. This isn't an old law-dog worrying, Amos," Ira Stone said, "this is an old law-dog knowing about danger."

Stone was sitting in a large leather chair in the Supreme Court justice's office, chewing on a black cigar that had never been lit. "This Burleson cannot be ignored, and I'm sure that he has made contact with Dooley or some of Dooley's men. They have big guns aimed at you, judge, and Chance can stop them."

"I'm not minimizing this threat you talk about, Ira," Amos Stanfield said, and his cigar was lit and he was blowing billows of smoke into the room. "I've heard the rumors, too. That fool Spencer even threatened me, but do you really think it's that serious? Do you believe they would hire a killer?"

"You tell me, judge," Stone said. "First, just assume for a minute that Burleson has contacted Spade Dooley, and I'm sure you know Dooley's reputation."

"Indeed I do," Stanfield said. "I've put him away twice, I'm sure there are existing warrants, and him looking to assassinate me is frightening. All right, Ira, I can't go to Preston for Christmas, but you bring Jacob Chance back with you. I have tremendous respect for that man and what he's done for that beautiful little Golden Valley. If anyone can protect me, it would be Chance."

Memories of his time in Preston flowed for some time after Ira Stone left the office. He could still almost feel himself sitting in that little camp that Ben Stokes had set up outside the town, enjoying roasted beef, singing with that monster of a blacksmith, and hearing some of the tall tales that were told by the marshals that had come to back up Jacob Chance.

"Maybe I should take the time to go to Ben Stokes's little party. I'd like to see Sarah Jackson again, and that feisty little daughter of hers, and maybe even arm wrestle that blacksmith again." He would have to give up a full week in order to do that, a week that he might need to finish writing that majority opinion. "Every single person living in Nevada will be affected by what that opinion will represent," he muttered, "and it must be absolutely as perfect as I can make it. Can I give up a week?"

Whether a person ran a ranch or farm, lived in a community, prospected for valuable minerals, or operated a working mine, it couldn't be done without water, and in some way how that water was distributed determined how that life was to be lived in the high mountain desert known as Nevada. Rivers and streams flowed through hundreds of properties from their headwaters, and most in the Silver State's rivers ended in sinks in some valley.

What happened to that water on its run was at the essence of what Amos Stanfield had to write, and what he wrote would become the law. It was flawed water law that brought the issue before the Supreme Court, and after blistering testimony, it was a majority opinion that had brought major changes to how the waters of the state would be distributed.

"I can't possibly give up a week to traipse about the state just to see and enjoy the company of old friends," Stanfield said, relighting that chewed up cigar once again.

Chapter Three

"Are you sure that old fool is going to travel to Preston?" Burleson asked attorney Harold Spencer, four days before Christmas. They were in Spencer's rather ornate office located within walking distance of the new Capitol building. Spencer had poured each some good bourbon and had a sly grin on his cleanly shaved face when he gave that news to the blustery rancher.

Spencer wanted to be stylish, wearing velvet suits, starched shirts, high top button shoes, but it came off more slovenly than stylish. The suit coats never quite fit right, the high collars seemed wilted, and his shoes were more often muddy than shiny. He simply was not a dandy, but was dangerous because he was given enough money to buy danger.

"This would be the time to take him down." *Providence*, Burleson thought, knowing how desolate the road between Carson City and Golden Valley was. There was the mail stage from time to time and very few single travelers. "If you're sure, I'll contact Spade Dooley immediately."

"According to one of the men working at the Supreme Court, Stanfield told the cleaning staff that he would be gone over Christmas and to leave his office alone. And one of Doyle's deputies has been assigned to ride with the party."

Sheriff Micah Doyle could keep traffic flowing in the capital city, arrested his fair share of drunks, and was probably not capable of understanding the word conspiracy. The fact that a Supreme Court justice was writing one of the most important documents of the 1870s, had been publicly threatened, and was planning a two day trip in

Nevada's wilds, did not ring security bells was the true indication of the lawman's abilities. For one of Doyle's deputies to simply blurt out the time and destination of Stanfield's journey would have been called treason anywhere else.

"One thing to remember, Burleson, the retired marshal that lives in Golden Valley is a good friend of Stanfield's."

"Retired marshals don't mean much to Dooley." Nate Burleson laughed, lighting up his well-chewed cigar, blowing smoke toward the ceiling of Spencer's office, and indicating that his glass needed a refill. Burleson was a burly man, heavy in the chest and shoulders, thin in the waist and hips, and his gnarly hands had immense strength. He had worked cattle from the time his father stole his first one.

"That mail stage leaves tomorrow morning, so I'd best get moving in order for Dooley to be where he would make his play. You earned your pay on this one, Spencer." He downed the bourbon and marched smartly out of the office.

The Silver Star Saloon and Dance Hall sat on Carson Street, directly across from the U.S. Mint, built in 1866 to handle the incredible amounts of gold and silver blasted from the fabulous Comstock mines of Virginia City, just fifteen miles to the northeast. The mint was made of stone quarried just outside Carson City where the state prison was located.

The new depot and passenger facilities for the railroad was less than half a block north. The Virginia and Truckee Railroad had brought new commerce, new vitality to the capital city, bringing ore from Virginia City to mills along the Carson River, and then bringing great bars of gold and silver to the mint, there turned into coins of the realm.

The Bank of California and others had pushed hard for that railroad, to serve the mills along the Carson River, but the plans were to push the line north from Carson City and join with the intercontinental Western Pacific in Reno. There would be a direct rail connection from San Francisco to Virginia City.

Burleson fought his way through the maze of construction, the tremendous flow of traffic that developed because of a combination of mint and railroad activity, and slipped into the Silver Star, an ornate saloon that operated around the clock, with gambling tables, ladies of shaded honor, and some of the finest cigars available outside Virginia City.

The barmen wore brocade vests, always had spanking white aprons wrapped about, and customers were guaranteed a welcoming smile. During the week, a free lunch was offered, featuring sliced cold meats and cheeses, fruits when they were available, and freshly baked breads and sweet cakes and pastry. The Silver Star was the center of the city's attractions outside the Capitol stuff, the barmen liked to say.

Richard Robinette, recently of San Francisco, was a partner in the Silver Star and oversaw the gambling tables. He picked up the sobriquet 'Dirty Dick' one evening when he was caught attempting a bit of sleight of hand dealing some five-card. His cousin, Silas, acted as saloon security and doubled as a paid gun riding with Spade Dooley and his gang, and that was who Burleson was looking for.

Silas Robinette, who had spent time in Micah Doyle's jail, usually for petty robbery and violence toward his fellow man, was standing near one of the tables watching his cousin deal when Nathaniel Burleson approached. Burleson nodded that Silas should join him at the bar, and the large man ambled over. Robinette stood slightly less than six feet and weighed a solid two hundred pounds. His arms were long and strong, and his hands were broad with long fingers.

Along with hiring out his ability as a gunslinger, Silas was an expert knife thrower, taking great pleasure in demonstrating his abilities at every opportunity. He was as adept at the undersling and side-arm as he was at the overhand throw, and the daggers he carried often doubled as shaving instruments. It wasn't a show, they really were razor sharp.

"Ride out to Dooley's and give him this," Burleson said, handing a heavy canvas bag to the gunman. "He needs it as quick as you can get it to him, and be prepared to ride when he does get it. Hurry now," Burleson said, adding a ten-dollar gold coin to the offer. Robinette left immediately, but before mounting his horse, he checked inside the bag.

"Well, well, will you look at this," he murmured, fondling the leather pouch stuffed with gold coins, and glancing at the map with the route the mail stage would take from Carson City to Preston. Robinette didn't read, so he was unaware of Burleson's instructions to Dooley. He was also unaware that Dooley was expecting there to be one thousand dollars in the large canvas bag when it was delivered.

It was a cold morning, a wind from the north starting to kick up, and billowing clouds making their appearance over the Sierra Nevada. Nevada's old-timers could feel a winter blizzard was just hours away. Carson City, located in Eagle Valley, was built along the front range of the Sierra and those mountains often had as much as twenty feet of snow over a winter.

Robinette rode hard through the Empire area, along the still almost new rail lines of the Virginia and Truckee Railroad, and found the Dooley camp along the Carson River, about eight miles out of town. "Brought you this from Burleson," he said, handing the bag to Dooley.

Dooley noticed the bag had been opened, found the map not folded properly, and quickly assumed that Robinette probably also managed to massage some of the double eagles nestled in their leather pouch. Spade Dooley rode for the Union in the big war, was a sniper of the first order, rode for Texas following the war, and rode for himself since. There are many who insist that he was riding for himself during the war and in Texas, as well.

He would take a lot from a man before striking back, but stealing gold from him was an automatic death sentence. He made a quick count and Robinette realized what he was doing and tried to back away some, ready to jump on his horse at the first sign of a problem. Robinette was wearing a heavy winter coat that hung well down his legs, split in the back for riding, but belted solid. He knew he could not reach any weapon, pistol or knife.

"Seems a bit light," Dooley said, his eyes squinting some, as he hefted the pouch in his left hand.

He gave the pouch a little swing, diverting everyone's attention to it, pulled his revolver and put a .40 slug through the middle of Robinette's chest. "Bury that fool, boys, then gather your gear. We're riding. Somebody find my hundred dollars on the stupid man. Dirty Dick will pay for his cousin's disrespect."

Spade Dooley led four men south toward the Golden Valley and Preston, figuring they would make their play somewhere near some alkali flats that lay along the trail. It would be about the half-way point, and desolate. He grinned. "No survivors, gentlemen. And don't leave any evidence that could point anyone our way. After, we will split up and not be seen riding together until well after we return to Carson City. You'll get your shares when the judge is dead. Let's go."

They stopped briefly along the way and pilfered a buggy and horse, some clothing, and some extra food from a rancher and his wife. Dooley didn't even take the time to have the bodies buried. "That storm is coming down on us fast, men, and we have some preparations to make. Nobody will even know these peasants are missing until spring." He snickered. Most of the men that rode with Dooley feared him more than they respected him. There was no compassion, no warmth of any kind for anyone or anything.

Many stories were told of his ability to kill without an ounce of remorse, of taking delight in watching someone shake and scream with fear, and then see the smile that crossed his face when he did make the kill. The stories out of Virginia City about Bad Man Sam Brown and his exploits were fairytales compared to Dooley's background.

"There's no reason to believe that Stanfield will have protection, but it doesn't matter anyway. Whoever is on that stage must be dead. If we meet people along the way, they must die. We cannot have anyone alive that knows we have been on this road. If you have any questions, speak now," he snarled. Not a word was said as they mounted for the rest of the ride south.

***

The stockyards in the Carson Valley were just about empty as winter made its way across western Nevada. Snow boiled off the Carson Range of the Sierra Nevada, and Hank Adams was holding a meeting of employees in the customers' lounge, a large meeting room where many cattle and horse auctions also took place. "Jake, you and Sam offered to hold down the fort while the rest of us take a few days off for Christmas. We want to thank you for that." Most of the employees shouted their thanks, and some playfully jeered.

"There's plenty of feed for the few animals we have on hand, and plenty of wood and coal for the stoves. We all thank you for that," and they got another good round of hoorahs and clapping.

"I made arrangements with Molly Malone at the hotel to fix you boys a big Christmas dinner, and she'll include a little bottle of brandy with it." Jake and Sam laughed at that and the rest of the crew gave them another round of clapping as well. "I'm heading back to Golden Valley, to sign new contracts for next year's herds, and eat as much as I can get in me. Let's be back to work on January second, and make this place ready for our spring calves.

"Speaking of this next season, it looks like the Virginia and Truckee Railroad will be expanding considerably. That line from Carson City to Virginia City is very busy, mostly hauling ore to the mills along the Carson River, but lots of merchandise, including our beef, pork, and lamb up that long hill," and he got some snickers from that.

"They will finish the line connecting Carson City to Reno and the Western Pacific Railroad this next year, and everyone's talking about running a rail south to Minden, right in our back yard. We will have direct access from our stockyards to Reno, San Francisco, Chicago, hell, boys, New York City." It took a minute for that to be understood.

"We're not in competition with the Chicago stockyards by a long-shot," Adams continued, "but we are for everything west of the Rocky Mountains. We'll be processing many more tons beef, lamb, and pork because of those long steel roadways. How's that for a Merry Christmas?" Along with the busy stockyards there was a mill in operation in Minden, and the Virginia and Truckee Railroad would be a busy line.

They ate rolls and pastries, smoked meats and fish, pies and breads, drank from cups, some filled with brandy, some with whiskey, others with coffee, wished everyone Merry Christmas, and the stockyards were closed for the season. Adams made his way back to his office to put what papers he would take on the stage tomorrow into his valise, and made the twenty-mile ride to Carson City to spend the night at a hotel. The stage left promptly at seven in the morning. The carriage was brimming with boxes of Christmas delights to be spread among friends in Preston.

Hank Adams was a burly former cowboy who found himself fully involved in the Golden Valley land and water fraud problems back in '62, when U.S. Marshal Jacob Chance rode to the valley and cleared out the criminal element. Adams rode with Cotton Phelps, Ben Stokes, Jerrod Stockton, and the marshals that came to Chance's aid, and after the fighting, when there was peace in Golden Valley, put together a coalition of the ranchers and farmers to move their produce and animals to the large market in western Nevada.

There were twenty thousand people living in the Comstock area, many more thousands in the capital city, and that new railroad town, Reno, was growing fast. After acting as an agent for the ranchers and farmers in the Golden Valley, Adams saw the need for a full-service stockyard operation, including buying and selling stock, but butchering and distributing as well.

Maybe I'll send a little Christmas greeting to William Sharon and his Bank of California boys for the gift of that railroad. He chuckled, wondering just how big his new market really was.

Adams walked into the restaurant at the St. Charles Hotel on Carson Street, on the other side of the street from the Capitol building, and found Amos Stanfield waiting for him. "I got your message, Amos. This will be a real pleasure sharing a coach ride to Preston with you. I'll be so glad to see everyone again. Jacob wrote that Ben Stokes will have enough meat on the fire to feed most of Nevada."

"It's been a long time since I was in Preston last," the judge said, memories of those days billowing out in his mind. "Preston could very well have vanished if that Sarah Jackson woman hadn't called for help. Everything was a fraud, the land sales, the water rights, the bank, and so many people dead or injured. They almost burned the town right to the ground.

"And just look at that little town today. There's a new bank, a real one,"–the judge snickered–"and a newspaper, good strong businesses, big ranches and farms, and men like you put it together, Hank."

"Nothing we could do until Jacob Chance and the marshals arrived, judge, and then you took over after all the battles and led the way. We'll have something to talk about on this adventure, tomorrow." Adams laughed.

They talked and reminisced all through supper and finally Judge Stanfield said he was calling it a night. "I'm gonna have a little after-supper snifter over at the Silver Star, I think, before I tuck myself in," Hank Adams said. They shook hands, Stanfield taking his little black buggy home, and Adams walking north for a couple of blocks and crossing over to the Silver Star.

The wind was howling and the snow was coming by the blanket-full as he made his way down the street. "Better make sure I'm dressed for this, tomorrow," he said, seeing Carson Street change from a muddy lane to one covered in white. "This is the water that everyone's fighting about," he thought, "and why our cattle are so fat and healthy."

Despite the late December storm and late hour, there was a fair crowd in the saloon and gambling hall. Dirty Dick Robinette was dealing faro at a filled table, other gamblers were playing cards at a couple of tables, and the bar was about half lined with men, some in working garb, some in business suits.

"Must be cold out there tonight," the barman said as Hank walked up. "You're bundled for a norther, I think."

"There's ice in that wind, Percy," Hank said, opening his great buffalo coat. "Better set me up with a nice snifter and bottle of good brandy." He looked around at the gaudy appearance of the saloon, with great chandeliers sparkling their crystals with gas lamps, an attempt at holiday celebration by way of pine boughs and wreaths with bells and ribbons, and the piano man pounding away at the ivory.

"Don't see Silas, Percy. He taking Christmas off?" Hank Adams laughed at what he considered a morbid joke. Silas Robinette had never been known to smile or less, celebrate some holiday or other. He took his pleasure in banging other people's heads and protecting his cousin's interests.

"He left out this morning and haven't seen him since," the barman said. "Dirty Dick's asked about him several times. Probably sittin' under a tree, drunk." The man laughed, knowing he would never say anything like that if either of the Robinette's could hear.

Adams chuckled softly, enjoying his brandy, watching the crowd, thinking about the long ride south in the morning. He had several boxes of gifts that he was bringing, for Cotton Phelps' family, for Jacob Chance's family, for Jerrod Stockton and his new wife, Eileen, and for Preston's sheriff, Jose Alvarado and his wife, Maria. "I'll need every inch of that stage coach," he muttered, "just to get all that stuff down there. Hope Amos isn't doing the same thing."

***

It wasn't quite dawn when Stanfield brought his little buggy down to the stage stop, filled with boxes to be transported to Preston. Hank Adams showed up shortly with his many boxes. Stage driver Dusty grumbled for half an hour getting everything loaded and still making room for his passengers. "Supposed to haul mail, you understand," he snarled, and then laughed and said, "Merry Christmas to y'awl."

Along with Judge Stanfield and Hank Adams, there was a young woman, tall, extremely thin, her complexion wan, almost waxen, and a man dressed in buckaroo gear. He was tall and wiry, with a head full of loosely curled and rather long red hair. He wore a buffalo coat like Adams', chaps and spurs, and when he said, "howdy," he was very obviously from way down south somewhere.

"Name's Slim Crockett," he said, handing Dusty his saddle and gear. "Got a job with a man called Cotton down in Golden Valley. Never been this cold in my entire life." Stanfield judged the cowboy to be no more than eighteen at best. "Been working cattle all across Texas and Mexico. Don't get cold there," he said, chuckling, tipping his hat to the young woman.

"Let me help you, there, ma'am," he said, offering his hand as she stepped into the coach. "Step might be a bit icy." He offered a hand to Judge Stanfield who almost cuffed him, but then smiled and said thank you, getting on board. Stanfield sat next to the woman and Adams and Slim Crockett sat across from them.

Dusty climbed onto his perch and took up the reins, gathering his four-up, and moving out onto the street. "Let's go boys, it's gonna be cold and long, and then cold some more." He hollered at the teams, putting them in a strong trot for the long ride to Preston.

"I'm Amos Stanfield," the judge said to the young lady, "and this is my friend Hank Adams. We're heading for a big Christmas celebration in Golden Valley. What brings you out in this foul weather?"

"I'm pleased to meet you," she said, lowering her eyes slightly. She too had a way down south accent. "My father lives in Preston and we're getting together for the first time in many years. I'm Clementine Bullis, my father is Justice of the Peace Roger Bullis."

"Well, for heaven's sake," Hank Adams barked. "So, we learn something else about old Roger, eh? That's wonderful news."

"He was hurt so bad in the war, and when mama died he just got on his horse and headed west. I didn't know where he was until just a few months ago. It took me a while to get everything in order so I could be with him."

"He's got himself a limp, Miss Bullis," Hank said, "but it doesn't slow him down too much. Does he know you're coming?"

"I hope so." She smiled. Demure was a good word to use for Clementine Bullis, and all three men genuinely enjoyed her smiles. "I've sent him a couple of letters. I've been working in Washington since the war and I don't know how long it takes mail to get way out here."

"Just about as fast as we're moving right now, miss." Judge Stanfield laughed. "All this talk about railroads, and I guess they're working, but it still takes a long time for us in the west to know what's going on in the east. I think the Pony Express was faster than these railroads."

Hank Adams laughed. "Gotta keep up with the times, judge. That beef that Chance and Phelps are shipping to me ends up being served at hotels in San Francisco and Salt Lake City because of those railroads. And that gold and silver brought down from the Comstock and turned into coins at the mint gets spent all over the country because of those railroads."

Stanfield laughed. "So you went to work for Stanford and company, eh, Hank?" That brought laughter from everyone. Stanfield couldn't help notice Slim Crockett taking sidelong glances at the lovely Miss Bullis. "You'll be arriving in Preston just in time for an annual Christmas wingding of a party, Miss Bullis. There's not a town in Nevada that can throw a party like Preston does."

Chapter Four

Virgil Thompson rode into camp at a fast clip, jumped from his horse and ran to Dooley's tent. "Stagecoach is comin', Spade," he said, breathing hard from a fast ride. "Better get ready." Like Silas Robinette, Thompson's specialty was knife work, and he usually carried an assortment, such as stilettoes, daggers, and Bowie, and was proud of his efficiency.

Spade Dooley came out of the tent, motioned for his gang to mount up, and ride fast toward the flats, about half a mile distant. They had set their camp in a stand of salt brush on the far eastern side of the alkali flats. Because of the storm, there was no chance they could be seen from the trail. The stagecoach could be carrying more than just passengers, and Dooley was hoping there would be cash and gold moving between the capital and the new bank in Preston.

"We'll make this look like a robbery and the fact the judge just happens to be a passenger was his hard luck," Dooley reminded everyone. "I want their money, watches, and jewelry, and if we're lucky, boys, we'll find a strongbox as well."

The wind was howling across the broad open plain, with most of the snow never reaching the ground, but traveling horizontally at about sixty miles per hour, in air that registered close to zero degrees. Dooley had the men hide their horses in some coolies, brought over the wagon they had lifted on their ride, and tipped it over in the middle of the trail.

One rider, Long Nose Jones, in a huge bearskin long coat and floppy hat, stood near the wagon, next to a dead horse, and waited for his 'wife' to join him before the stagecoach arrived. Jones was wearing a pair of Navy revolvers and carried a rifle as well. Chip Adler, dressed as a frontier woman, but holding a double barrel shotgun under his heavy winter coat, joined his 'husband' next to the dead animal. Both were giggling like little children.

Spade Dooley and Virgil Thompson, chuckling at the sight as well, hid down in the gulley with the horses, and waited. "We'll let Chip and Long Nose make their play and then jump up and join them. Remember, now, no survivors."

***

"It's about as cold as I ever want it to be," Slim Crockett said through chattering teeth. The stage was rocking in the wind, and despite the lowered curtains, the blizzard was fully involved inside the coach, snow swirling through in gusts that threatened to overturn it. They could hear Dusty yowling at the four-up, trying to keep them in a steady trot that would eat up the miles.

"We won't make Preston this evening," Hank Adams said. "There won't be many places to get out of the wind, so plan on spending a long cold night in the coach. I'm sure Dusty will keep the horses moving, at a slow walk for sure. If anyone can get us through in this weather, it's old Dusty. He's made this run for eight, maybe ten years, and knows the country better than the local Indians."

They heard Dusty start to yell at the horses to slow down, felt the coach begin to slow, and Adams and Crocket both grabbed for the curtains, getting them rolled up. As the coach moved through the heavy blowing snow, they saw a wrecked buggy, a horse lying in the snow, and a couple waving furiously for Dusty to stop.

"That's a nasty wreck," Adams said, getting ready to jump from the coach to help. "Judge, you and Miss Bullis best stay in the coach. Slim, you come with me." They slipped out from under the heavy wool blankets that were spread across their laps and covered their legs, and got ready to jump out as the coach came to a stop.

A blast from a shotgun and a scream of death from Dusty, and Hank Adams jumped from the coach, hit the ground and rolled toward the side of the trail. Slim went right behind him, hearing the pop, pop, pop from a revolver, but not feeling anything.

Adams got as low to the ground as he could, and saw the woman of the couple pull that shotgun in his direction. He leveled his rifle and drove her back ten feet, dead. The man of the family pulled a rifle up and Slim fired twice with his big Navy, hitting the man in the leg, tumbling him to the ground. He wasn't out of the fight, though, and rolled toward the dead horse, to use it for protection.

Spade Dooley and Virgil Thompson clambered out of the gulch on the other side of the coach from where Adams and Crockett were, and made their move toward the passengers inside. Thompson was met with scatter shot from a ten-gauge carried by Judge Stanfield, and was flung back into Dooley who whirled and tried to dive before the second barrel was fired.

Dooley scrambled on hands and knees to find protection behind the dead horse, pushing Long Nose Jones out of the way. Adams had jumped up and ran as hard as he could around behind the coach and, using the gulley for cover, moved to where he could see the men behind the horse.

Slim Crockett fired two more rounds toward the men behind the horse, not hitting anything, but drawing fire. While Long Nose Jones fired at Crockett, Dooley put three fast rounds into the coach, hearing a scream from inside. Hank Adams took a long slow squeeze on his trigger and sent a big chunk of lead through Dooley's chest, taking him out of the game.

"You're the only one left alive, Mister Stupid," Adams howled through the storm. "Toss those weapons and step out where we can see you." He waited what he considered more than enough time for a sensible man to make the right decision, and put three fast shots into the area where he figured the lone gunman might be.

"Okay, okay. I'm comin' out. Don't shoot no more," Jones yelled.

"Throw the guns out or die," Adams barked, and watched as weapons were tossed into the snow. "Good boy," he said. "Now, come out slow and easy, with your hands where we can see them."

Jones put his hands behind his head and stood up. "Don't shoot," he said again. His right hand closed around a throwing knife he wore where it could be brought into a fight fast. He walked right up to Adams who saw the challenge before Jones could pull the knife. A bullet tore through Long Nose's chest, ending the fight at alkali flats.

"What was that scream from the coach," Slim Crockett said, jumping to his feet and racing to the coach's still open door. He found Clementine Bullis being attended by Judge Stanfield.

"She's hit bad," Stanfield said. He ripped more cloth from her dress and used it to pack a wound to her leg. The bullet seemed to enter just above the knee and ran up and deep into her leg. Hank Adams joined Crockett, took a quick look, and drew Crockett back outside.

"We're in deep trouble, cowboy. Have you ever driven four-up?"

"I can drive teams, Hank," he said. "Learned in Texas."

"Good. I'm going to take one of these outlaws' horses and hightail it to Preston just as fast as that horse will run and bring help back. I need you to drive the coach at a moderate speed. Just stay on this trail as best you can. Even with all this snow it shouldn't be that hard to see it."

Hank stuck his head in the coach and told the judge what the plan was, grabbed one of the horses, and lit out for Preston. Slim Crockett climbed up to the stagecoach seat, rearranged Dusty's body, gathered the reins, and got the coach back on the road. He nudged the horses into a gentle trot and braced himself for the icy gale that assaulted him. *I thought Texas was full of rough people. Sure didn't plan on any of this*, he grumbled silently, keeping his head tucked down low into that big buffalo robe coat. *That little girl sure was nice looking. I hope she ain't hurt bad. She goin' to Preston and me gettin' a job there, well, I might just want to know more about her.* Thoughts like that kept the young Texan warm, to a degree: the cold was intense.

Stanfield had his hands full doing what he could to ease Clementine's pain, and stop the blood flow. "I want you to take a little taste of this, miss," he said, unscrewing the lid to his brandy flask. She took a sip, almost gagged, but got it all the way down.

"That's horrible," she squeaked through her pain, bringing a chuckle to the judge.

"Might be, but it will help. It's a nasty wound, but I've got the blood stopped and we'll be in Preston soon," he lied, knowing it would be many long cold hours before this rig would make it. "Have another little bit," he said.

***

"It feels like I'm about forty miles out, maybe a little less than that," Hank Adams muttered, putting his horse into a fast trot, fighting his way through deep drifts, and blowing snow. "This surely isn't a good cow pony," he said, feeling the sluggishness from the horse. "What I need is one of Jacob Chance's good strong range horses." With fresh and drifting snow he knew he didn't have to wrap the horse's feet. "Won't be cuttin' through ice on this trip, just everything else old Mama Nature might throw my way."

He had to put the horse into a walk after about every half hour of trotting to let the horse blow and get its strength back. He was caked in ice and probably frozen to the saddle, when he finally rode that poor horse into Preston. It was just coming sunrise, he noted, meaning he made that forty miles or so in about twelve hours. "With so many stops for this poor old nag, we're lucky we made it at all," he growled.

He rode right up to Stockton's Blacksmith and Livery and woke Roger Bullis up. Together they found the doctor and got him up, explaining the problem during the time it took for the doc to get dressed. "We need to meet that stage, doc, so you can mend that lady's wounds. She was shot bad."

"I can't believe my daughter's actually gonna be here. Doc, you gotta save that girl," Bullis said. "I'll get good horses saddled, Hank. Bring the doc to the stables," and the old confederate soldier limped back to the livery.

"I haven't seen Clemmy in so many years," he murmured, getting two horses saddled and bridled. He picked two of the strongest, both off the Chance string. "I wonder if she'll even recognize me. Come on, doc, hurry," he said, seeing the doc and Hank run into the big barn.

Hank Adams and the doc mounted and rode off into the gale wind and heavy snow, putting their strong horses into a fast trot, both men bent into the face of the blizzard. Adams had already spent twelve hours in the saddle and was worn out. It was only his background of constant hard work that gave him the stamina to make this second long ride. There was no let-up in the storm, and now they were riding head first into the full frenzy of a Nevada blue norther.

"Stay right with me, doc, and we'll be fine," Hank Adams howled through the wind. Doc Macy didn't say anything, but did put his horse right alongside Hank's and stayed right with him. Macy was a small man, wiry is how those that knew him said, and in good physical condition. Around town, the man was dapper in his dress, but Cotton Phelps could testify that when they were hunting together, the doc was a gamer.

"I'll be fine, Hank, but let's not kill the horses trying to get there fast." He tucked his chin deeper into his heavy blanket coat and tried not to let his teeth chatter.

***

"You'll be fine, Miss Bullis," Judge Stanfield said, pulling a bloody pile of rags from the wound and applying a new dressing. The blood flow had been reduced considerably and the judge wondered if it were the bandages responsible or if the dear girl was just running out of blood. He feared the worst. *She was so pale to start with, I sure hope she's strong enough to last through the rest of this night.* After about the third sip of brandy, Clementine had refused any more, and Stanfield smiled, taking a taste for himself.

The coach was being blasted by incredible gusts of wind, rocking back and forth, and Stanfield felt certain more than once the coach would simply tip over, but it never did. He smiled when he heard that cowboy, Slim Crockett, howling at the horses, just as loud and profane as Dusty used to do. "Get us there, safe, cowboy," the judge murmured.

"It hurts," she whimpered, as she regained consciousness. "What happened?" She tried to sit up and was shot through with pain, letting herself lie back, pulling the wool robe closer around her head.

"I'm afraid you've been shot, miss," Stanfield said, taking her hand and rubbing it gently. "We're still moving toward Preston and there is help coming to us as well. You've lost some blood, but the bleeding has stopped, and I think you'll be fine. Old Doc Macy should be able to patch you up just fine." He wasn't sure he really believed that, but it was important for her to believe it.

"What is it about Preston that it seems to be in so much turmoil at all times?" He snickered, thinking about the last seven or eight years. "All that ruckus with those fools trying to make people believe they owned the entire Golden Valley, and Jacob Chance fighting 'em off in grand style. Then, that crazy German, what a fool he was.

"I wonder who those people were that tried to hold us up?" Because all Judge Stanfield was able to see was a man and woman next to a wrecked buggy and dead horse, and then the shotgun blasts. It never occurred to him that it was a planned assassination. His assassination. "What a strange place to plan a holdup."

***

Slim Crockett wasn't sure he was going to be able to keep going much longer. The cold was seriously affecting his ability to think; he was shivering so violently that he could hardly keep hold of the reins, and found he was no longer able to yell at the horses. He realized they had slowed to a walk and they gave every indication they would rather be standing still.

He, too, simply wanted to lie down and go to sleep, and had to fight with every ounce of strength he had left to smack the reins onto the drivers' rumps, give one last rebel yell, and get the horses moving. Moving back into a solid trot, the horses felt the warmth of working blood move through their bodies and began to work hard again, but Slim wasn't so lucky.

He put slack in the reins, wrapped the ends around the brake lever, and started slapping himself across his own face, whupping his shoulders, stomping his feet, even trying to jump up and down, almost falling from his high perch, and finally began to feel the warm blood pulsing through. He took the reins back up, smacked the drivers a good one, and felt much better.

The long night slowly turned into day, but the storm seemed to get even stronger, with gusts of wind hitting the stagecoach so hard that Slim was sure the wheels were off the ground more than once. He had to slow the horses to a walk often, they were so tired from plowing their way through immense drifts, fighting incredible winds, and not getting any rest. The drifts were hub deep in some places, and Crockett had lost all feeling in his hands, feet, and face, and knew he could not go on much longer.

***

The only reason the reins were still between his fingers was they were frozen there, Hank Adams said when he climbed up on the seat next to Slim Crockett and broke the reins free. He eased Crockett off the seat and down to Judge Stanfield and Doc Macy. The two then got the almost frozen cowboy inside the coach and under some wool blankets.

Adams had the two saddle horses tied to the back of the coach, climbed up to the seat and goaded the team into moving again, while doc and the judge started work on the two patients. "Well, young lady, you're sure gonna have some fine stories to tell that father of yours." Doc Macy smiled, getting his little black bag opened, and looking at the wound for the first time.

The bullet had entered at an angle and stayed inside the leg, not bursting through, and Macy knew he had to get it out, and knew too, the lady could not tolerate that kind of pain. *It's only because of the cold that she isn't already facing blood poisoning. I hope she's half as strong as that father of hers.* He had nothing with him to ease the pain, either. "Don't s'pose you have a nip of barley corn with you, judge," he asked.

Stanfield started to give off a big harrumph and then caught the doc's meaning. He reached inside his heavy coat and produced a second flask that was almost full, pulling the stopper and handing it to Macy.

"You need to drink some of this, Miss Bullis," he said, tilting the flask to her lips. She tried to fight him, but he insisted, and she took too large a sip and coughed mightily for a few minutes, and doc urged her to have some more. It wasn't long and she was woozy enough, he figured, that he could at least probe about some and find that bullet.

It was on the back side of her upper thigh that he felt the bullet through her skin, gave her a couple more good nips of Judge Stanfield's finest Kentucky bourbon, and proceeded to make a deep slash into the thigh. Clementine Bullis passed out from the pain and Doc Macy produced the bullet on his first probe. He chuckled. "She'll hate me when she wakens, but she won't die of blood poisoning." Macy took a hefty slug of the fine bourbon before handing the flask back to Stanfield.

With her wounds cleansed and wrapped, Bullis slept soundly the rest of the way into Preston. Stanfield, Macy, and Crockett sipped down the rest of that fine bourbon just as the coach pulled up next to Stockton's Livery. "Glad you saved me some," Adams snarled when he found out the flask was empty, but Roger Bullis saved the day, producing one of his own.

"Thank you, Your Honor," he said, with a slight bow, and drank mightily.

Crockett was the first out of the coach and helped Adams lift Clementine Bullis out. "There you are, miss, not quite as good as when we started this little journey." Crockett smiled, holding her upright. He had his arm tightly wrapped around her waist and they went into the stables' office. Roger Bullis was right behind.

"Clemmie." He was almost crying when Slim put the lady onto the cot near the red hot stove. "It's really you. My God, it's really you," and the tears flowed. Slim Crockett produced one of the heavy wool blankets from the coach and they tucked her in. She smiled at her father, looked at Slim Crockett and gave him a big smile, closed her eyes and slept. Crockett's heart was pounding from the smile, Bullis's heart was pounding at having his daughter home.

Chapter Five

"You're absolutely certain of that, sheriff?" Stanfield asked when Jose Alvarado returned to Preston with the four bodies. "If one of those men was dressed as a woman, and if that dead man there really is Spade Dooley, then that was not an attempted stage coach robbery. Those men were sent to kill me, and I'd put a lot of money into believing Nate Burleson paid for the attempt."

Jacob Chance nodded his head, fully understanding the threats he'd been told about were real and Stanfield was in serious danger. He'd spent his career in the Marshal Service protecting judges, chasing criminals, protecting the rights of citizens, and knew that his decision to return to Carson City with the judge was the right one.

It was the day before Christmas and there was anything but peace and goodwill flowing through the streets of Preston. They had to bury old Dusty, who had been a mainstay in the community for so many years. "That man drove wagons here once a month for years, and then started bringing the stage. He never gave the weather a second thought, helped beat off attempted holdups, and never failed to make his run," Jerrod Stockton said at his funeral.

The four assassins were buried after every attempt was made for identification. Their personal belongings were in a pouch with letters from the sheriff and justice of the peace addressed to the Ormsby County Sheriff in Carson City, to be returned on the next stage out.

The storm had reduced itself to a brisk breeze coupled with periods of snow flurries, and the two big questions being debated at a back table at Tiny Bidwell's Crystal Saloon was whether the weather would allow for

Ben Stokes' Christmas festival, and what to do about an assassination attempt on Judge Stanfield.

Included in the conversations were discussions about Roger Bullis's daughter, Clementine, arriving in town, and whether or not she would survive that terrible bullet wound. There was considerable talk about the new cowboy looking to ride for Cotton Phelps, and whether he would survive frostbite, dehydration, and a serious case of love sickness. Crockett had spent as much time at Clementine's bedside as old Doc Macy.

Nevada State Senator Jerrod Stockton was presiding, and those participating included Supreme Court Justice Amos Stanfield, retired U.S. Marshal Jacob Chance, Preston Sheriff Jose Alvarado, Preston Justice of the Peace Roger Bullis, Ben Stokes, Cotton Phelps, and Hank Adams.

"I have one question, Amos," Jacob Chance said. "Why did you leave Carson City without some kind of protection if you knew there had been threats? I know just how strong willed you are, sir, but this is your life we're talking about." Chance was beside himself when he found out the judge traveled without protection.

It was the solemn duty of the U.S. Marshal Service to protect federal judges, and even though Stanfield was a Nevada jurist, the state should have provided something. "Hank and Crockett saved the day, but somebody in Carson City should be looking for a job if I have anything to say about it."

"I know how you feel, Jacob, and I was a little concerned when the deputy sheriff that was assigned to travel with us didn't show up, but we did get mighty lucky to have that young cowboy along for the ride." He added a touch from a bottle of Kentucky to the coffee cup on the table, and got a nice smile from Tiny behind the bar. Stanfield continued. "Micah Doyle, the Ormsby County sheriff, assigned a deputy to ride along, but whoever that was never showed up."

The word conspiracy shot through Chance's mind and he saw the same look in Hank Adams' face. "You don't suppose that deputy was purposefully detained, do you?" Chance snarled. "I see a determined effort to eliminate you, judge, and it's past time for you to understand that. To have a buggy overturned, to have a gunman dressed as a woman, and all of this in the middle of a December blizzard, tells me this was a well-planned execution. Thankfully Hank and Crockett were along."

It was a solemn group that understood just how close the Dooley gang came to pulling off the assassination of Stanfield. "I'm expecting Ira Stone to ride into town at any minute, judge," Chance said, "and when our Christmas party is all over with, he and I, along with Hank and Jose here, will give you a proper escort back to the capital. I will be staying in Carson City and will be your shadow until there are no longer fears for your life."

"I had that conversation with Ira," Stanfield nodded with a little grin. Ira Stone, formerly a U.S. marshal, had been the U.S. attorney for the state of Nevada for several years, and was in on the cleaning up of Preston years ago. "I found that there is a budget item for protection of the justices, Jacob, so you will be compensated for your efforts to keep me alive for a bit longer."

"Well then," Ben Stokes piped up, "with that little project taken care of, let's talk about a Christmas Party," and gentle laughter spread around the table. "If the gods of winter will let up just a bit, I see no need to postpone our little shindig. We'll cook the large items, such as a side of beef or two and the venison, over the outdoor coals, and everything else in those large stoves in the house and the bunkhouse. Any objections?" he asked.

"The women have suggested that we serve and eat inside that large bunkhouse," he said. "Buckaroos are already setting up barrels with planks laid out on top for tables, so we'll seat probably thirty at a side, and with two tables stretched the length of that building, we'll have plenty of room."

The talk continued for another hour or two and broke up when Ira Stone rode into town, almost as cold and wet as the group that arrived on the stage. "You can make it for another couple of hours, Ira," Chance said, insisting that the two return to the ranch immediately. "If Jennifer finds out I left you in town I'd be looking for a new home." He laughed. "I thought you were bringing your new wife?"

"I almost said to hell with it, myself," Stone said, sipping some more of the judge's good whiskey. "She's a plucky young lady, Chance, but I simply could not let her face this kind of journey. The only reason I came is because Stanfield needs the two of us, Jacob. I want you to bring me up to date on that mess out on the road."

***

Burleson rode into Carson City from his large ranch in the Carson Valley and stormed into Harold Spencer's office, bullying his way past the receptionist. "Well?" he thundered. "What has Dooley said? Is our problem taken out?"

"No one's heard from Spade Dooley, and Silas Robinette is still missing, too. I did manage to get that deputy drunk as a skunk and he did not ride out with Stanfield, but there's been no word back from anyone."

Burleson paced around the office, stood by a large set of windows and looked down on a snowy street filled with people preparing for their Christmas holiday. Almost every buggy, wagon, and cart was decorated for the season, trees were being hauled in constantly, and groups of singers walked about celebrating and caroling. All of the gayety frustrated the rancher even more.

"That man must die, Spencer. He must not be allowed to write that opinion, it must not become law," he thundered, chomping on his cigar. "Send riders out and find

Dooley. Find out what happened, and in the meantime I will put together a new plan. For the time being we will have to assume that Stanfield is still alive, which means he will be back at his desk in two or three days, maybe four at the outside.

"This law must be written by the legislature, Spencer, and you will see to it." He continued pacing for a minute, and then stormed out the door saying something about the Silver Star Saloon. Spencer sat back in his chair wondering why the rancher didn't simply send a couple of his cowboys out to search for Dooley. He motioned for his secretary to come in.

"Ted, we need to know what happened to Spade Dooley. He should have been back in town yesterday. Send a couple of riders south and see what you can find out. Keep it quiet, there's no reason for others to know why you're sending the riders out."

Ted Whistler was in his early thirties, reading law, acting as Spencer's secretary, and more often than not was treated as a lackey more than as a student of law. "I'll get right on it. You have a hearing at one, and the sheriff asked that you stop by when you get a chance." *I'm within a year of being an attorney at law and I'm working for a criminal. I've embarrassed myself enough, I think. When Justice Stanfield returns, I'm going to speak with the man. It will probably end any possibility of me becoming a lawyer.*

***

"Join me for a drink, Robinette," Burleson said, strolling near the gaming table held down by Dirty Dick Robinette. Burleson had a bottle of whiskey and two glasses, and took one of the tables near the back wall at the Silver Star Saloon. He immediately lit a cigar and poured healthy shots of whiskey for the two.

"Heard anything from your brother?" he asked as Dirty Dick sat down and took a drink. Robinette scowled at

Burleson, understanding that his brother hadn't been seen since the rancher sent him on a mission of some kind.

"No, Burleson, I haven't, and if he's hurt or dead, I believe you are responsible. You tell me where he is."

"I paid him to take a message to Spade Dooley," Burleson snapped back. "Maybe he rode out with Dooley. It certainly wasn't a dangerous little job," he smiled. *Unless the fool got greedy and got into that leather purse filled with gold.* "I need to put a couple of tough hombres to work, Dick. A couple of men who might not have much use for the law, and who might not mind if the work involved hurting or killing someone. I'll pay well, and you'll get a nice fee for the job."

"There're always men out of work, Burleson. How many you thinking of?"

"Probably no more than three. You get me those men in three days and you'll get yourself a hundred dollars each. Don't let me down," he said, downing his whiskey, getting up and marching out onto Carson Street.

"You are one foul person, Burleson," Dirty Dick snarled, pouring another shot and drinking it. "You're one dead man if I find out you're responsible for Silas not coming back from your little job." The muttering continued for another two shots of whiskey and Robinette got up and strolled to the bar.

"Sammy," he said to a short, heavyset man standing near the end of the bar. "You still looking for work?"

"Mines are laying off people, not hirin' them," Sammy Lauck said. "Whata ya got in mind?"

"Friend of mine is looking to eliminate a little problem. Might take two or three big strong men who know their way around guns and knives. The job would be dangerous but the pay would be good."

"How good?" Lauck's eyes had narrowed some and a slight smile crossed his face, while visions of gold coins danced about. The prospect of making good money in the middle of a bitter Nevada winter had him riled up a bit.

"Can't give you an exact figure right now, but if you put together a nice bunch to hit that little problem of my friend, I can send you to the man who will tell you how much. I need an answer in two days, Sammy."

Chapter Six

Jennifer had a table set for a king that night, with roasted leg of lamb, potatoes, green beans, and fresh bread. "Ira, you're simply going to have to come to supper more often if Jenny is going to cook like this for you." Jacob Chance laughed, slicing great slabs of meat for the eager diners. The children had challenged Ira to arm wrestling. Little Jake, seven years old and very large for his years, showed himself well. Missy, four years and counting, was just a bit frightened by this new man with the huge moustache and growly voice.

Table talk dealt with Ira Stone getting married after all these years, and the political atmosphere in Carson City. "The word within the Marshal Service, Mr. Chance," Ira said, "is simply this. If Jacob Chance can find a woman crazy enough to marry him, anyone can. So, I did." He laughed. "She's not a ranch girl, Jenny, more citified I think, and enjoys Carson City."

Settled into large armchairs that Ben Stokes had built as an anniversary gift a couple of years ago, proving the old man still had all his background skills working for him, Ira Stone and Chance got right down to business. The stagecoach affair was proof of just how much danger Amos Stanfield was in, and how difficult it would be to protect a man who tended to shun the concept of protection.

"Before we get all involved in the big Christmas shindig at Ben's, you need to tell me everything you might know or think might be important about this plot to kill Amos. That stagecoach hit was well planned, Ira. Well planned."

"They knew when and where, Jacob, there is no doubt. Spade Dooley's gang has been involved in some serious crimes around western Nevada and the nearby Sierra Nevada communities, and I've heard rumors that Nate Burleson was looking to hire him for a job.

"It's Burleson who is behind the major effort to not let the Supreme Court publish their water rights decision before the legislative session. If Stanfield does not publish the decision, and the legislature passes their convoluted law, the Supreme Court decision will be meaningless. Burleson and some of his land-owning cronies, along with some of the mine owners, are getting desperate."

"It's a state's rights thing, Ira, so I guess that leaves you out of the game, federal marshals would be out of the game, and that leaves local law enforcement. How does Micah Doyle stand on this?" If Chance were going to be guarding Stanfield he would need the backing of the sheriff, and what he heard at the saloon that morning wasn't favorable to such backing.

"Doyle is a simple man who was elected because he smiled to the ladies, promised to keep the drunks in line, and bought drinks at the bar," Ira Stone said. "He does not see the problem, Jacob, at all. I'll give you as much help as I can, but don't expect anything from our good sheriff.

"Burleson's attorney is a slimy little jerk named Harold Spencer, and it's Spencer that set up Dooley with Burleson, and I would bet it was Spencer that saw to it the deputy did not make it to the stagecoach. I have two federal investigations underway, one on bank fraud and one on mail theft, with Spencer high on my list of suspects. He's a slimy back stabber, Jacob, so visit him first."

***

It was bitter cold on Christmas but with help from several, Ben Stokes had roasting fires going early and meat turning on spits, the ladies all turned out with side dishes, pies, bread, and fruits. Chance estimated at least fifty people joined the celebration, and once again the singing was led by Jerrod Stockton. Even Judge Stanfield took part.

Chance brought Jennifer and the children in the buggy with a team of dancing young colts he was in the process of training. "It's good for them to get this kind of work," he said as they headed back to the ranch. "I have to leave in the morning, Jenny. Amos is most interested in getting back to Carson City as soon as possible."

"I know," Jenny whispered, snuggled up in a buffalo robe, as close to Chance as she could get. "I don't want you to, but I know you have to. I'll bring the children during the third week of January, and we'll stay through the legislative session, or at least some of it."

"I'll stay at the St. Charles until you come and then we'll take a small house. It will seem like half of Preston will be in the capital, with Senator Stockton, Hank, Cotton Phelps, and us. Don't worry, my pretty, I'll stay safe." He knew just how dangerous this would be, dealing with people who have no use for the law. He left just before sunrise for the ride into Preston.

***

"It's doubtful that anyone in Carson City knows that the attack on you failed," Chance said to Stanfield as they got him, Ira Stone, and Roger Bullis settled in the coach, armed to the teeth. "We should have an easy ride back, but we'll stay sharp, my friend. You'll be safe."

"I know I will, Jacob. Thank you isn't enough, I know, but it will have to do for now."

"Roger, are you sure you want to come along on this ride?" Chance asked the war veteran/justice of the peace. "Is Clementine feeling well enough to take care of herself? That was a nasty wound she suffered."

"She's doing fine, marshal," Bullis answered with a smile. "There's a certain young cowboy that seems to spend more time caring for my daughter than working for Cotton

Phelps. That boy is in love, marshal." He laughed, settling in under a heavy wool blanket.

The new driver, a fellow called Ornery Jones, spit a wad of tobacco juice half-way across the street, took up the reins, spread some most profane language, and the four horses stepped out smartly, with Chance, Hank Adams and Sheriff Alvarado riding their horses along.

"I'll take point," Chance said, "a couple of hundred yards out front, sheriff, you ride about that far behind, and Hank, stick close to the coach. At least there's fair weather for our trip. Old Slim Crockett sure wanted to come along, didn't he?" Chance laughed. "He's a game young man. Hope Cotton Phelps can keep him on."

"It'll be Clementine Bullis that will keep tabs on that young'un." Hank Adams laughed.

"If he doesn't work out with Cotton Phelps," Alvarado said, "I'll hire him for my deputy."

***

The stage pulled into Carson City two days later having not the least bit of trouble on the ride. Stanfield had his cart hitched and Jacob Chance rode with him to his home on the west side of the city, near where the new governor's mansion was being planned. It was a stately Victorian home, two stories and a carriage house off to the side and toward the back.

"Who do you have living here, besides you?" Chance asked, as he helped the judge carry his carpetbags and a couple of boxes into the home. There was a fire burning hot in the fireplace, and the smell of fresh coffee was evident.

"My law clerk, Augie Roark, rooms here, Jacob. You'll like him, he's big, bright and, he tells me, ready to fight for me anytime." Roark came into the living room carrying a tray full of cups and a large pot of coffee.

"Welcome home, Justice Stanfield. Hope you had a good journey and a merry Christmas." Jacob was looking at a man of about twenty-two or so, with black wavy hair, and bright green eyes. He stood almost Chance's six feet plus and weighed another twenty-five pounds heavier.

"There have been no stories about Judge Stanfield's trip south?" Jacob asked.

"No," Roark answered. "Should there have been?"

"Indeed, there should have been, Augie," Stanfield answered. "Say hello to one of my oldest and dearest friends. This is retired U.S. Marshal Jacob Chance. Chance, say hello to Augie Roark, my law clerk."

Roark beamed. "What a pleasure. I've heard some wild tales about you, sir," and the two shook hands. "I sure hope you're here to keep this gentleman safe and alive."

"That's exactly why I'm here, Roark, and I'm glad to see you're a man capable of helping should the need arise."

Chance stayed through the pot of coffee and they brought Roark up to date on the failed attack on the stagecoach and the death of the Dooley gang. Roark said there hadn't been a word about it in Carson City.

"There will be, soon enough," Chance said, slipping into his heavy bearskin coat and floppy sombrero. "I'll be staying at the St. Charles, Amos. Stay home and I'll be here first thing in the morning to escort you to your offices. Take good care of this man, Mr. Roark," and he walked out into the cold of a winter's afternoon.

***

"Who was that tall man with Stanfield?" Burleson asked. When the stage arrived in the capital city, Burleson, Spencer, and Spencer's law clerk and secretary were on hand to observe. There had been no word from Dooley, and it was a surprise to see the Supreme Court justice step out of the coach, very much alive and well.

The Christmas storm had left a thick blanket of snow over the city and was now melting, leaving a sea of mud in its place. Getting from one side of the street to the other was a feat for the brave. If one didn't slip and fall in the mud, then a horse or wagon would surely cover you with it. When the sun set, the mud would freeze solid, leaving great canyons down the lengths of the streets where wagon and buggy wheels burrowed in.

"That, my friend, is the man you must be very wary of. He's Stanfield's friend, retired U.S. Marshal Jacob Chance. The Mexican is Preston's sheriff, Jose Alvarado, you know Hank Adams, and I don't know the man with the limp.

"Just a guess, Burleson, but a good one. Dooley and his gang are either dead or they're in jail in Preston. Dirty Dick Robinette sent Sam Lauck to see me about putting together a group. Your idea?"

"You bet it's my idea. I will give one thousand dollars to the man that kills Stanfield and I will give Robinette one hundred for finding that man. We're running out of time, Spencer."

***

It was not a long ride from Carson City to Virginia City, but it was steep in places and the traffic could be heavy. The mines on the Comstock were belching silver and gold by the ton and wagonloads of the precious metal were moving downhill while wagonloads of merchandise for the multitudes that lived high on Sun Mountain moved uphill.

Traffic was a little lighter now that the railroad was running and so much of the ore was going down to the mills along the Carson River. Visitors, dignitaries, and the nabobs of the mining district rode in splendid railroad carriages.

Sammy Lauck had been fired from several of the operations and knew his way around Virginia City's criminal district, along C Street's south end. He left his horse at the Pioneer Livery on B Street, walked down Taylor to C, and then south for about a block. "Robinette set me up for a good job, I think," he murmured, "and I surely could use some of that thousand bucks right now."

He finally found the man he was looking for at the Golden Wheel and motioned for him to join him at one of the tables. "Good to see you, Tony," he said when the man came over and sat down. Tony Martucci was a big, powerful man, about five ten but weighing in at close to two hundred pounds. His specialty was shooting his man in the back.

"I got a job for you and Johnny Ferris if you want it. There's a man in Carson City needs to be eliminated and I'll pay three hundred for the job. That would be one fifty for each of you. He's an old man, might have an old retired marshal acting as security. Should be an easy pop."

Johnny Ferris was a weasel in every way. He would scam his mother if a gold coin was involved, worked crooked card games daily, and was deadly with his Henry, or with a knife. Ferris and Martucci were well known to the Virginia City law dogs, and the Committee of the 601 had them on their list as well.

"Make it four hundred, Lauck, and fill me in. I'll find Ferris and I know he'll do it for two hundred. Would this be that judge that everyone's talking about? He put me in the slammer when he was a district judge. This will be my pleasure to whack that old bastard."

"His name is Amos Stanfield and he's a justice on the state Supreme Court. There are ranching and mining interests that want him eliminated right away. Spade Dooley was supposed to make the hit, and what I heard, they hit him instead, so here's a chance for you to really make a name for yourself."

"I got a name, Lauck," the gunman said with a questioning look on his face. "You got a plan or should I just get it done?"

"He's all yours, Tony. You and Ferris handle it your way, and when it's done, you'll have your gold." Lauck finished his beer and walked out of the saloon, and took Taylor Street one more block downhill to D Street, turned north and headed into Virginia City's line-up of cribs filled with lovely ladies of the night. With Martucci and Ferris on the job, he could almost feel that thousand dollars in his pockets.

***

The word of Dooley's death spread through the capital city, and talk of the attempted assassination of Stanfield was on everyone's lips. Virginia City reporter Mark Twain was in Stanfield's office the next morning to get the story. "The entire fight was over with inside of a minute, Twain," Stanfield said. "Hank Adams and that young cowboy, Slim Crockett, seemed to react as if they had done that a hundred times. It was amazing."

Twain was about to leave when Jacob Chance walked into the office. "Ah, Jacob, here's someone I want you to meet. Say hello to Mark Twain. Twain writes for the *Territorial Enterprise*, in Virginia City. I just gave him the story on how the Dooley gang went down."

"I've read some of your fables, Twain." Chance chuckled, shaking hands with the young reporter. "And some of your actual news stories." Twain, too, chuckled and nodded goodbye to the judge and Chance, and headed out the door. The reporters on the *Territorial Enterprise* often wrote 'tales' and slipped them into the news columns, which caught some in the east unaware. More than one eastern reporter had come west to follow up on one of their tales.

"Tell me about this Harold Spencer, Amos. I got a cryptic message from a man named Whistler who works for Spencer and wants to meet with me for lunch."

"Whistler is a young man studying law and clerking for Spencer. He also acts as Spencer's secretary. Spencer is the attorney representing Nate Burleson who is the man who wants me dead. I'm relatively sure it was either Spencer or Burleson that hired Dooley, and I would be careful dealing with Whistler. He's too close to Spencer. I'm not sure that he understands how he may be hurting his chances of becoming an attorney."

Chance left the court building and strolled down Carson Street toward a café for his meeting with Ted Whistler. The law clerk was seated toward the rear of the café with his back to the door and front window. Chance took the seat across from him and saw a large man, well groomed, but with sadness in his eyes.

Carson City, unlike so many towns on the frontier, was growing up, and this café told that story. It was bright, well lit, large windows facing the busy main street, with homey decorations on shelves, and bright colorful paintings of local scenery dotting the walls. The women that owned and worked in the business dressed as if they were ranch or farm wives, in pretty gowns, even wearing well decorated hats from time to time.

"So, Mr. Whistler, what is this mystery you wished to discuss?" Chance said, getting right to the point. Chance had given up the serape and floppy sombrero for a well-tailored buckskin jacket and no hat, and looked the part of a successful Nevada rancher. "This attorney you work for doesn't have the finest reputation."

"I'm very worried about that, marshal," the young man said, taking a quick look behind to see if anyone might be watching. "Mr. Spencer might be involved in something that could ruin my career before it even gets started, and might lead to the death of a good man."

"If you're alluding to Justice Stanfield and what happened with the Spade Dooley attack, you might very well be right," Chance said, sipping on some hot coffee. "I can't prove Spencer hired Dooley, but I'm working on that."

"I can prove that Burleson hired Dooley through Spencer, and that Spencer just arranged for another man to kill the judge. I have to get out of this mess, marshal. I can give you everything I know if you'll help me get out. I'm not a bad man, don't want to be a bad man. I thought clerking for Spencer would help me become a better attorney, but it's seemingly going the other way. He's teaching me how to be a crook and a killer."

Chance smiled a bit at that, saw the irony in Whistler's face, and understood the man's situation. "You've been drawn in and you want out," he said, getting a vigorous nod. "I can probably help you with that. Tell me everything you know, in writing. The Preston sheriff, Jose Alvarado, and Preston's justice of the peace are heading back to Preston on the stage this afternoon.

"You be on that stage and they will give you all the protection you'll need, and I'll take Mr. Spencer out of the game. All of this will be to your good record, Mr. Whistler, and I'll see to it."

Whistler handed a large envelope across the table to Chance. "Everything is in here, names, dates, bribe offers, the hiring of guns, everything. I'll never be able to thank you for this, marshal."

"You're doing the right thing, Whistler. I'll see to it that Stanfield knows just how much you have contributed to Spencer's downfall. The only name besides Spencer's that I've heard is Burleson. Who else might I be looking at? Other ranchers? Others in town?"

"Burleson makes the most noise, but the man you want to be most careful of is a rancher named O'Brien, Seamus O'Brien. His ranch is in the northeast section of the

Carson Valley, and he's not a nice person. Another rancher is Henry Carrington, and another would be Thomas Bigler. They all visit Spencer regularly, and bring him large sums of money. It's all in that envelope."

"You've done your job well, Whistler. Time now for me to keep you well." Lunch was fast. Chance nibbled on a piece of tough boiled beef, suggesting the café should buy Preston beef, and read through the documents, asking questions, making sure he understood everything the man had written. They walked to the stage office in time to meet with Alvarado and Bullis.

"You take good care of this man, Jose," Chance said. "Mr. Bullis, this man is studying to be an attorney, so maybe you can let him read through all those books you've been getting every month." He suggested that Alvarado ride out to the Chance ranch and deliver a note to Jenny, saw the stage off, and carefully looked through the small gathering to see if anyone was especially interested in the passengers.

Back at Stanfield's office, Chance laid out the documents for the judge. "Mr. Whistler is doing the right thing, Amos," he said. "I've shipped him off to Preston where he'll be safe. According to Whistler, Sam Lauck has hired a couple of Virginia City outlaws to kill you. I'm leaving for the Comstock now and should be back in a day or two."

It was a quick walk to the V&TRR yards where Chance boarded the train for the ride to Virginia City. The line ran through what had been a beautiful canyon that was filled with mills to handle the hundreds of thousands of tons of ore being mined on the Comstock. Those mills needed the water from the Carson River, and it was the mining and mill owners and operators that formed the company that built the railroad, with a little help from the Bank of California.

The road's initial purpose was simply to haul ore down the mountain and goods up the mountain. It quickly became a success as a general-purpose railroad. Chance took the time on the trip to go over again and again what Ted Whistler had given him. "This is so much more than just a conspiracy to murder Judge Stanfield," he kept murmuring. "This Burleson seems to think he owns the legislature, and if he doesn't get his way, those standing in his way must die."

Chance watched the landscape change rapidly from the lovely Eagle Valley to the long river canyon, then starting the steep climb to the Comstock. There were tunnels to pass through, and one long, very high, trestle to roll across. *Like criminals everywhere, these men only think of themselves, have no use for others, and don't give a hoot who they might hurt, as long as they get their way. Spencer is in my sights right now, using the law to commit a crime.*

Chapter Seven

Chance was given a room on the third floor of the extravagant International Hotel in Virginia City and had a list of names that he needed to follow up on, including the Storey County sheriff and Virginia City police chief. The same man held both positions. "For a young man, this Phineas Byrnes seems mighty capable," he mused. "I think I'll pay that man a visit first."

Virginia City is built on the side of Mt. Davidson, often called Sun Mountain, with major north-south streets terraced up its flank. The connecting east-west streets are very steep and in the winter, with icy conditions, hazardous to man and beast. The International Hotel had a main entrance on C Street, and second main entrance one street above, on B Street. That entrance was on the second floor of the grand hotel. The International catered to the elite of the Comstock, and San Francisco.

Many of the mine owners and stockholders lived in the city by the bay, and with a railroad connection, the men enjoyed visiting their properties. Oysters and champagne flowed from silverware that was once directly under where the hotel sits. Some of the Comstock mines were more than one thousand feet below the surface.

Directly across B Street stood the magnificent Piper's Opera House, and just half a block to the south, the Storey County Courthouse. Chance stepped carefully down the snow-clogged street and found Sheriff Byrnes at his desk glancing through wanted posters. "Morning, sheriff," he said, stepping into the office and shaking that huge bearskin coat off. "I'm Jacob Chance and we need to have a bit of a talk."

"Marshal Chance," Byrnes said with a smile. "I've certainly heard my fair share of stories about you. Sit down, sit down. Have a cup of coffee?" Chance was looking at a big man, probably still in his late twenties, robust in build, with a fair complexion. His light hair was a bit longer than Chance would wear, but neat, and the man's intense blue eyes seemed to sparkle.

"Thank you, yes, I would. A little too much work, being county sheriff and city police chief?"

Byrnes laughed some, pouring the coffee and sitting back down. "There isn't much else to Storey County except Virginia City and Gold Hill. There are a couple of small ranches, a few small coyote hole mines, and that's about it outside of town, so the sheriff part of the job doesn't entail much. But I can tell you the chief of police is busy." He chuckled. "I heard about the attempt on Stanfield. Is that what brings you to town? I thought you were retired from the marshal service."

"Yup on both points, sheriff. I promised Stanfield protection, and I am retired so I have no authority other than that of a citizen. The attack on his stagecoach last week was well planned and I have serious evidence of a second plot that's about to happen involving some residents of Virginia City." He took a large drink of the hot coffee, pulled an envelope from inside his shirt and handed it across the desk.

"This is from the law-clerk working for an attorney in Carson City, Phineas, putting names and places together."

"Phineas is my name, Chance, but everyone calls me Hawkeye." He snickered a little. "Picked that up when I was a kid down in Texas. I could hit a running quail with a rock in my sling faster than Papa could hit it with a shotgun. Squirrels were my favorites, though." He got serious and business-like, opening the envelope and paging through what Ted Whistler had written.

Chance watched as Byrnes' face changed from jovial to serious, from questioning to understanding. *I like this kid,* he thought, taking some more coffee. *I hate to admit it, but he's a lot like I was at that age, so serious at times, and so full of it at other times. I hope we get to work together.*

"Lauck, Martucci, and Ferris, eh? Ferris is deadly with that Henry of his and Martucci has never looked a man in the eye during the killing. Prefers the back. Not so dangerous, you understand," he said with a growl and a grin. Chance found the man's humor interesting and saw another side of Hawkeye Byrnes that he liked even more. "Lauck is a slimy little bastard, Chance, and it will be my pleasure to find him tucked into my little jail.

"Martucci is big and strong, but has the coward's way about him. I've tried to pin more than one death on the man, but he's a bit too sneaky to leave me good courthouse approved evidence," and the snicker rolled out with the irony. "Ferris is the one that will put up the biggest straight on fight."

"Good to know all this, Byrnes," Chance said, not willing to call the man Hawkeye, just yet. "I won't get in your way, sheriff, but I do hope I have your backing in bringing this attempt on the judge's life to an end."

"Yes, sir, Marshal Chance, you have my backing all the way," Hawkeye Byrnes said, standing and shaking his hand. *To work with Jacob Chance, U.S. Marshal? And he asks if he has my backing? My God in heaven I could dance on the desk right now. All I've ever wanted is to be a good lawman, honest, strong, brave, everything that Chance stands for, and now I will be working with the man.*

Hawkeye Byrnes was born on the border in El Paso, Texas in 1845, troubled times he was told, but the family got out and ended up near Santa Fe in New Mexico. The Mexican American war was raging, but the area became New Mexico Territory in 1846, and the family stayed for several years. They returned to Texas following the war, and Hawkeye grew up on a hard-scrabble Texas farm.

Looking at Marshal Chance brought some memories back. He remembered being in trouble a lot, getting caught stealing chickens because there wasn't any food in the house, getting caught stealing other things because he wanted them. And getting the tar beat out of him by that Texas Ranger, Silas Grundy. *It was Grundy that changed my life, damned near crippled me doing it, but I'm a better man because of him.*

He was a friend of his father, this Captain Silas Grundy, Texas Rangers, who encouraged the young man to find a career as a lawman. "You've got good gravel in your craw, boy," he told the young man, "so put it to good use." Hawkeye Byrnes moved north through Kansas and Iowa cattle towns and during the war years was hired by the Army of the Potomac to hunt down and arrest those fleeing the fight.

After the war, it was back to cattle country and into the plains, railroad towns, chasing rustlers, and just a year ago he found himself elected sheriff in Virginia City, Queen City of the Comstock.

Now just look, he pondered, *I'm going to be working right alongside Marshal Jacob Chance. I wonder what old Captain Grundy would say about this?*

***

Johnny Ferris was at the Sazerac Saloon waiting for Sammy Lauck to show up when Tony Martucci walked in and joined him. "Heard about the marshal coming in?" he said, pouring a shot from Ferris's bottle. "Somebody named Chance came in on the train last night. I heard he works for Stanfield."

"He's just an old marshal that runs a ranch somewhere, Tony. You believe everything you hear? He ain't been a marshal for years. Lauck'll be here shortly and we can plan on how to kill that judge. That money's as good as ours, so don't be getting yourself all riled up about some washed out marshal."

Martucci had heard stories before about Jacob Chance, U.S. Marshal, and knew what Ferris was saying wasn't right. He also knew that Ferris did not like to be contradicted, would lash out when he was, so he sat quietly, thinking about the problem. "I think we should get the judge late at night at his big old house in Carson City, Johnny. He lives far enough out of town that we wouldn't draw no notice."

"Yeah, that would be good, Tony. Maybe also we could think about getting him when he drives that buggy or one of his fancy two-wheel carts into town in the morning." They took another slug of whiskey as Lauck came in and joined them, filling his glass too.

"A couple of little changes, boys," he said, putting the empty glass back on the table. "Spencer's man, Whistler, gave us away to a marshal. Marshal Chance knows our entire plan and Spencer wants us to get out of Nevada as fast as we can. The deal is off, boys. I'm heading for Sacramento as fast as the train can get me there." He took another shot of whiskey, got up and started for the door.

"No you ain't, Lauck. You still owe us some money," Martucci snarled. "Maybe we didn't finish the job, but we started. You owe us some of what we were working for."

"There was no job, Martucci. Ferris, tell your idiot friend there was no job, therefore there is no money." He was standing near the table, his hand hovering very close to a big revolver, probably a Walker, hanging from a heavy belted holster, glaring at the big man.

"Well," Johnny Ferris drawled, "you did in fact hire us to take out the judge, and we had every intention of doing just that. Now, you say, the hit is off, but that doesn't mean that we didn't do some of that job. I think you owe us some of that money, Sammy Lauck. Yes, I do believe Mr. Martucci is right." All the time he was talking, Ferris was slowly letting his hand get as close to the handle of his big Colt as possible.

Martucci stood up quickly, giving Lauck the wrong impression, and his Walker was up and out of that holster, cocked, and flashing fire and lead so fast that Ferris didn't have time to pull his pistol and found himself looking down the barrel of Lauck's. Martucci was flung backward, crashing into another table and falling to the floor, mortally wounded.

All the action in the little saloon stopped at once, men at the tables holding drinks or cards were statues, and the men at the bar didn't budge. Blue smoke slowly cleared as one of Byrnes' constables came running into the saloon with his weapon drawn. "Hold it right there, Lauck," he said. "Lay that gun down on the table, slow now. Don't make this worse than it already is." Lauck knew the man was behind him and would kill him in an instant, and did what he was told.

The constable sent one of the men in the saloon to fetch Byrnes and disarmed Ferris, letting the barman take care of the weapons. "Sit down," he said to Lauck and Ferris, and took a close look at Martucci to make sure he was dead. "You first, Lauck," Constable George Martin said, "what brought all this about?"

"We were discussing something and Martucci got angry and jumped to his feet to kill me," Lauck said. "I simply defended myself. This is self-defense, Martin."

Martin looked at Ferris and said, "Well?"

"Pretty much what he said, but I'm not sure Tony was really going for his gun."

Martin thought the same thing since Martucci's revolver was still snug in its holster, but didn't say anything. "Chief'll be here shortly, so just sit and be quiet until he gets here. Don't nobody touch that body until Byrnes says so." Martin took Martucci's weapon up to the bar and then started taking statements from the men who were drinking at the time.

Byrnes came at a run from the courthouse, made his way through the always very heavy wagon traffic on C Street and into the Sazerac. "What have we here?" he said to Martin, surveying the mess.

"It looks like Lauck pulled a gun on Martucci and shot him dead. Martucci's revolver is still in its holster," Martin said. "I talked with most of the men here and they agree that Martucci never went for his gun.

"All three men were in an argument of some kind."

"What was the argument about?" Byrnes asked Ferris and Lauck.

"Business," Ferris said, Lauck nodding agreement.

"What kind of business?" Byrnes shot back.

"Personal," is all Lauck said.

Jacob Chance walked in and Byrnes waved him over. "Glad you're here, Chance. This is Sammy Lauck," he said, pointing the man out, "and this is Johnny Ferris. The dead one is Tony Martucci. You wanted to meet with these gentlemen, I believe."

Chance smiled at Byrnes' humor and nodded. "According to a wire I just got from Nevada's federal attorney, Ira Stone, Mr. Spencer was attempting to close his office and run off to San Francisco a couple of hours ago. I assume you gentlemen were discussing the fact that you were no longer in his employ, and your plan to take out the judge was over and done with. Am I correct?"

Neither man responded, but Chance caught Ferris taking a quick look at Lauck, then looking down at the floor. "Something on your mind, Ferris?"

The outlaw shook his head, and continued staring at the floor. Lauck was sitting, staring at his two hands, folded on the table.

"What have you got, sheriff?" Chance asked, not taking his eyes from Ferris.

Byrnes spelled it out quickly, and suggested that he and Chance should have a quiet conversation away from Lauck and Ferris.

"Keep an eye on these two, Martin," Byrnes said, wagging his finger at them.

He and Chance walked over to the bar and had the barman pour a couple of cold glasses of beer. "I've got Lauck on murder, for sure, Chance. Martucci never made a move for his weapon, just acted stupid and it cost him. What do we do about Johnny Ferris? He's not involved in Martucci's death, but certainly is involved in the conspiracy to kill the judge."

"Unless you can prove that they were discussing that conspiracy, sheriff, that question is out of your jurisdiction. The Nevada attorney general has all the information on that, but hasn't initiated any warrants. Right now, Ferris could walk out of here and disappear.

"One thing, you could hold him as a material witness to a capital crime, but only until tomorrow afternoon. I would let him know just how much you know about the conspiracy, just how much the AG knows, and talk about saving his neck. It's your game, sheriff."

"I think I'll hold him for questioning and ask you to wire the attorney general and see if he will issue a warrant. We can't go beyond that. He's guilty as sin of being hired to kill that judge, but until a move is made, there's no crime I can arrest him for."

"No, there isn't, but the crime of conspiracy is there, and you can hold him until Elmer Barlow makes his decision, grill him lightly, threaten him gently, and suggest that things would go easier if he told you everything." Chance wanted to do the grilling and threatening, but he was not able to. "Right now, it's your ballgame, Hawkeye."

These are the times he missed most from his old life. He was thinking how much he enjoyed being a rancher, watching his cattle herd grow, seeing his horse program working out, but missing these times. *Hawkeye will have Lauck begging to confess and that sneaky little bastard Ferris will have tears in his eyes when that boy gets through with him.*

How many times and in how many different situations had he had big bad criminals on their knees begging him to stop his questioning, giving it up in spades, as he used to tell the federal judges. *I'll never go back, never give up what I have, but I have to admit I do miss a lot of my old life.*

***

Ira Stone and Amos Stanfield were in the office of Elmer Barlow, Nevada's dynamic attorney general, discussing the situation when a telegram was delivered. "It's from Chance," Barlow said. "Looks like Martucci was shot by Sam Lauck and the Virginia City sheriff is holding Lauck and Ferris until I issue the warrants for their arrest.

"Anything of a federal offense in any of this, Ira?" he asked, hoping that federal charges could be added to the state charges. "Right now, all we have is conspiracy to commit murder of a state official. Those are serious enough, but federal would add to the list."

"The only federal case would be if Harold Spencer is able to get into California before we catch him. Crossing a state line to evade capture is federal, but I think the Washoe County and Reno people will have him in custody shortly.

"If I could be bold enough to make a suggestion, Barlow?" Ira Stone asked, and Barlow said anything would be welcome at this point. "You have an opportunity to put one of the finest investigators I've ever worked with on this case, working for you. This conspiracy involves people in several county jurisdictions, and you should be leading the investigation, not the local sheriffs.

"I believe that if you asked former U.S. Marshal Jacob Chance to take the lead and bring the conspirators to heel, he would jump at the chance."

Amos Stanfield smiled broadly at the suggestion, patting Stone on the shoulder. "That's a wonderful idea, Stone," the old judge said. "We've only been talking about Spencer and his hoodlums, but the real criminals are those behind the attempts on my life, those that do not want the Supreme Court judgment to be finalized. Chance is more than capable of bringing this to a conclusion."

Barlow pulled paper from his desk and wrote the warrants for the arrest of Spencer, Ferris, and Lauck, and followed it up with a wire to Chance in Virginia City asking him to escort the prisoners to Carson City and meet with him at his earliest convenience.

***

"This whole project is out of control, Burleson," Henry Carrington said. "We have the votes in the legislature to write this state water law the way we want it, where we have final say as to how much water we can use, whether it's water under our land or on our land. Now, we have an investigation underway at a high level that could put all of us in prison for a long time. I've said right along, the answer was money, buy that damn judge, and we didn't do it."

Six men, four ranchers and two ranch hands, were sitting around a large table in Nate Burleson's home in the Carson Valley. Word of Jacob Chance going to work for the state's attorney general had spread quickly through the western areas of Nevada. "This should have ended weeks ago, but Spade Dooley let us down," Burleson said.

"Nonsense!" stormed Thomas Bigler, whose ranch spread out south and east from Genoa, with a couple of miles of the Carson River flowing through his property. "Instead of simply bribing that old fool, Stanfield, you decided to be the bad man and hire gunslingers. We were against that from the start, and now look where we are. That water in that river is mine as soon as the river crosses onto my property, and I'll fight anyone who says different."

"The man wouldn't bribe, Bigler," Burleson said, quietly, as a beaten man might say. "You all agreed that we had to take Stanfield out, we all agreed, take out the judge, and so far, we have failed."

"You have failed," Bigler corrected, getting nods from the others. "Now we have Mr. Law and Order himself, Attorney General Elmer Barlow, hiring a U.S. marshal who has worked with U.S. Attorney Ira Stone, breathing down our necks. Spencer is in custody, Lauck and Ferris are in custody, and Spencer's own man turned on him and told this Jacob Chance everything we've tried to do. Chance may have our names if they were in Spencer's files. What else does he know?

"The question now, gentlemen, is almost simple. What the hell do we do?"

Orion Seamus O'Brien's ranch was in the northeast corner of the Carson Valley, some of the acreage spilling over into Eagle Valley, with more than two miles of the Carson River flowing through. "Unless Mr. Burleson was stupid enough to include our names in some of the correspondence he had with anyone, I'd say we just sit tight. Did you mention any of us in letters with the legislators, with Spencer, with Stanfield?"

"There is nothing on paper with anyone, gentlemen," Burleson said. "I have had no written correspondence with anyone. What Barlow and Chance have is from Spencer only, not one word from me. Spencer knows our names, but there is nothing in writing from me to implicate any of us. This question of names is up in the air, right now."

"Then," Carrington said, "Spencer must die. According to talk in Carson City, Spencer will be brought back to the capital later this week. He is being treated for a broken arm and twisted ankle right now. I have two cowboys just joined the ranch that would be willing to kill Spencer, for a couple of hundred each. I'll put up the first hundred." Bigler put up the second, and they all agreed that Carrington would take care of the arrangements.

"Even if we get the Spencer problem solved, there is still the judge," Bigler said. "The legislature is scheduled to convene during the second week of February and we are already in the middle of January. Stanfield cannot be allowed to formalize that opinion. Let's not lose track of our primary goal, to protect our water. That water does not belong to John Q. Citizen, it belongs to us, those of us that have that water on our property. It's there for us to use as we see fit."

O'Brien held back as the others filed out of Burleson's barn. "Nate, let's you and me have a little chat, eh?" He reached inside his coat and pulled a flask out. "This is straight from the Emerald Isles, my friend," he said, taking a nip and handing the flask to Burleson.

"Oh, that's fine whiskey, Seamus. What's on your mind other than what we've been discussing?"

"We've been creating these intricate plots to take out the judge, and I think all we really need is one man with a fine rifle and keen eye," O'Brien said. He cocked his head in a knowing way, took another sip from the flask, and continued. "I have a man works for me takes great pride in hitting jack rabbits and ground squirrels in the head at more than one hundred yards.

"I asked him if he could hit a man as easily at, say, two hundred yards. He waved an old Henry in my face and said he could do it at three hundred yards. He said if the price included getting him out of town, he'd be glad to shoot our old friend, Judge Stanfield." O'Brien took another nip of the Irish and handed the flask to Burleson.

"Everyone runs to Sacramento and San Francisco, Seamus. If your man was put on a coach east, this might work. Did he mention what that price might be?"

"He did, and I paid him. Only the three of us know this, Nate. I've not said a word to Carrington or Bigler. I want you to handle getting him out of town safely."

"I will. Is there a date?"

Orion Seamus O'Brien told Burleson that the man was making his plans and would let him know when he would make the hit. The two men lowered the level in that flask some more and had smiles as they parted.

Chapter Eight

Sean Dougherty was a cocky little Irishman who believed that he had never been beaten in any kind of fight, fists, knives, guns, or feet, and the Henry he carried had taken more than one man from the back, some from the side, and a few from in front. He had a passion for killing, his blood boiled at the thought of watching something die, and it mattered not whether man, beast, or fowl. When Seamus O'Brien approached him with an offer of five hundred dollars for knocking off an old man, Dougherty was slavering at the chance.

He spent two days looking over Stanfield's property, spent some time riding back and forth on the route the judge used going to and from work, and believed he found the exact spot to lay in wait. On the night before his planned hit, he slipped into a mangle of trees and brush some one hundred fifty yards north and west of Stanfield's, built a little lean-to of the brush and downed limbs, and crawled in to make himself comfortable. He brought some smoked meat, biscuits, and a flask of good Irish whiskey.

"They'll give me that five hundred, a ticket to Salt Lake City, and all I gotta do is pop an old man. Seamus O'Brien should be ashamed of himself for hirin' out a job he is fully qualified to do himself." He took a couple of solid nips from the flask and pulled the wool blankets tight and was fast asleep in minutes.

The night was cold and clear with just the hint of a breeze and no moon. From Stanfield's home it would be impossible to see Dougherty, and if someone did happen to ride down that gravel covered lane, he would be well hidden as well. Dougherty's dreams on nights like these always returned to his time with the Army of the Potomac and his sniper duties.

He could almost feel every kill, in his dreams he could feel the rifle's recoil, see the dead man, feel the thrill once again. He awakened several times that night, checking to make sure there was no one around his firing hole, took a swig or two of Ireland's best, and went right back to his dream world.

***

"Thanks for coming on such short notice, Hawkeye. I tried to get a message to Chance but he's out of town right now." Augie Roark had a worried look on his face when Byrnes stepped into the judge's office. "Justice Stanfield is in his inner office and I'd rather he didn't hear what I have to say."

"You look like a worried man, Augie. Has there been another threat?"

"I think so. For the last two days I've seen someone who doesn't live in our neighborhood and who I've never laid eyes on before, riding about with no obvious business." Augie Roark described the man, and what caught Byrnes' attention was the mention of a large rifle in a scabbard.

"Was there any particular place this man seemed to spend a little more time around, or seemed to have his eye on?" Byrnes was well aware of what a sniper with a fine rifle could do, and knew just enough of Stanfield's neighborhood to know that a man could make a nest well within range for a good shot.

Roark described two places in particular and Byrnes thought he knew what the man was talking about. "If you do find Chance, let him know about this right away," he said, shook the man's hand and made a quick walk to his horse. *That storm probably put some good drifts in that area,* he thought, *and that would lend itself to even better concealment. Damn snipers. Chance hasn't said anything about these people setting up this kind of hit. Must be something new, now that Spencer is in custody.*

He tied his horse at Stanfield's carriage house and stood for just a moment at the spot the judge might stand in the morning to climb into his favorite two-wheel cart, and looked around in a complete circle. "Right there," he said, looking at a stand of broken trees and brush, about a hundred fifty yards away, "would be my first spot. Full concealment and a clean shot, even if the judge moved over here," and he stepped away a bit, "or moved this way," and he stepped a different direction.

Augie Roark told Byrnes that Stanfield left the house at nine sharp, every morning, and that gave Hawkeye time to do some planning of his own. "If that sniper fella is gonna be over there, and I know he will be, then I have to be somewhere I can see him." He mounted and rode off as if heading for town, circled way around and came up on what he was now calling the 'sniper's nest' from behind. The sun was almost down, and the shadows were long and dark as he rode slowly down a slightly used dirt lane.

He could see the bank of busted up trees and brush and tucked his horse into a stand of quaking aspen and tied off. He started slowly moving toward the nest, keeping inside the line of trees along the lane. "If I was going to be making this hit, I would want to be in position a long time before sunrise. Get there early enough that I might even get a good nap." He chuckled.

He looked around the area, he was a good five hundred yards from the nest and was trying to figure out from where the sniper might approach his spot. "The man won't want to be seen, but will have to come by horse. He sure as hell won't just walk up with a rifle and blankets in hand. Bastard might come the same way I have." He snickered again. "Just walk right up to me," and he had to stifle the chuckles.

"Will you look at that." He snickered, seeing a man on horseback ride right past Stanfield's property and turn onto the lane that led to the 'nest.' He rode past the spot, and turned his horse into a stand of mixed aspens and pines about half way between the spot and where Byrnes was. The man tied off his horse and pulled the rifle from its scabbard. Byrnes recognized it as a Henry, even from that distance.

He had a bedroll and extra blankets, and saddlebags, probably filled with food and whiskey, and kept inside the line of trees and made his way to his nest. "Looks like I'm one lucky sumbitch tonight," Hawkeye mumbled. "I'll let that fool get all settled in, then I'll move up on him." Byrnes watched as night came on fast, and when he almost couldn't see his hand in front of his face, he crept out onto the open lane and moved toward where the man tied his horse off.

"I can't get much closer right now," he mumbled. "Damn snow has an icy surface and it's noisy." He pulled the saddle from the sniper's horse, just in case the man tried to escape, and tucked himself under some heavy brush for the long wait. He could see the nest, just before it came complete dark, and knew he would be able to get much closer later in the night.

Thoughts of Texas and family and hunting worked their way in as he curled up with his heavy buffalo robe coat. He loved walking into stands of trees, so slow his muscles ached, and spotting a squirrel, whipping that sling, and adding fresh meat to Mama's supper pot. He smiled, could almost smell that stew, and slipped into a nice sleep.

It was the wind blasting its way through the trees that woke Byrnes with a start. It took just a minute to focus on where he was and why, and he gave full attention to the sniper's nest area. The wind was making the aspen trees dance and he smiled when he realized just how much noise there was. He uncurled from the blanket coat, made sure his rifle was in perfect working order, and slowly advanced on the sniper.

Icy wind slammed into that heavy coat, and there were snowflakes mixed in it, which gave Byrnes a white covering too, and he made his way, one long slow step at a time, through the downed trees and brush, his eyes locked on the spot. It was just coming light, that period well before sunrise, and Byrnes was close enough that he could see what he knew had to be the sniper wrapped up in wool blankets. He was no more than twenty yards away and he tucked down behind some brush to wait for sunlight.

A particularly sharp gust of wind rattled the trees and Sean Dougherty came awake with a start, shook off the blankets, grabbed his rifle, and looked about almost as a scared squirrel might. Byrnes snickered. Dougherty fumbled around with the rifle, got the blankets cleared from him, and settled down. He unscrewed the cap from his flask and took a long drink, shook himself from its effect, and replaced the cap.

Wish I had some of that right now, Byrnes thought, and watched Dougherty build a good bench of snow with a wool blanket folded on top from which to shoot Stanfield. *This fool knows what the hell he's doing. Has himself a fine bench rest, and an open shooting field. Sure glad Roark spotted him or that judge would not have lunch today.*

As the morning wore on, the wind continued, with a few snow flurries flung about, and Byrnes was enjoying watching Dougherty take more hits from his flask. *That man's gonna be half in the bag when I take him to jail,* he murmured. He watched Augie Roark come out of the big house and walk to the carriage house, bring out the fine two-horse cart. As Roark harnessed the horses and brought them out to hitch them, Judge Stanfield walked out and down off the porch.

Sean Dougherty brought the Henry up and onto the bench rest, and snugged it up to his shoulder just in time to hear a voice say, "Freeze or die." Dougherty spun around and Byrnes put a bullet into the middle of his chest, chambered a second round, and shot Dougherty through the middle of his head.

Roark grabbed Stanfield and wrestled him to the ground, demanding the man stay still, and watched as Byrnes stood up and walked out from the stand of aspens, and waved at him that it was okay. "You're safe, judge," Roark said, getting up and off the old justice. "That's Hawkeye Byrnes out there."

Roark helped the judge to his feet. "Are you okay?"

"Probably bloody and bruised from you knocking me about, Augie, but I'm not shot or dead, thank you." He brushed himself off, got in the cart, and he and Augie Roark drove into downtown Carson City for another day of court work. "I suppose you'll take a few minutes out of your busy day to tell me what that was all about?"

***

It took more than an hour for Byrnes to get back to his horse and bring it up to the nest, get Dougherty's horse saddled and up to the nest, and then Dougherty's body and belongings onto that horse. He brought the body to the sheriff's office and spent another hour writing the report on the attempted assassination of Stanfield. He was just finishing up when Chance walked in.

"Good work, Hawkeye," he said, grabbing a cup off the hanger and pouring a cup. He sat down across the desk from his young deputy, frowning as he sipped the hot drink. "These guys just come up with one foul plan after another. Do you know this fool?"

"He's a drifter named Sean Dougherty, Chance. Been working for Seamus O'Brien, but I'm sure he isn't a cowboy. I'd be willing to bet he had some work as a sniper during the war. He made himself a fine sniper's nest out there, and if Augie Roark hadn't spotted him lurking around, Judge Stanfield would be dead right now."

"I just left Stanfield and he's still shaking like one of those aspen leaves you were hiding among. Maybe he'll take all this a little more serious now." He smiled, pouring the two of them some more coffee. "What did Micah Doyle have to say when you dropped off the body?"

"Tried to say it wasn't his jurisdiction but I played your game, marshal. I simply said it was and walked off to write my report."

"Good for you, Hawkeye. That's the way to do it. Now, my friend, we have one more report to put together. Let's go see Elmer Barlow at the AG's office and bring him up to date, visit Ira Stone and bring him up to date, and then I think Amos Stanfield owes us a fine lunch at the St. Charles Hotel."

Chapter Nine

"Do not let anyone get close to this man," the Washoe County sheriff told his deputies as they cuffed his wrists and chained the ankles for Harold Spencer's ride to Carson City. "There's a wagon with two-up waiting outside, with a driver. Chain Spencer in the back as well, and you ride fore and aft." Sheriff Watson had two of his best men riding guard and felt sure the trip would go without any problems. The driver had been told to stay on the main road, not take any shortcuts or make any stops on the thirty-mile ride to Carson City. "Stop for something to eat in Washoe City and wire me the minute this prisoner is delivered," the sheriff said, sending them off.

The first ten miles was through the southern wetlands of the Truckee Meadows, past numerous ranches, with considerable traffic on the road. They gave the horses a rest at what was called Brown's, where a toll road then traveled east toward Virginia City. They continued south for another five miles, past Steamboat Hot Springs, the attractive areas known as Pleasant Valley, across a ridge, and dropped into the Washoe Valley, stopping for a hot meal.

Lumber mills were scattered around Washoe Lake where great timber for the mines in Virginia City were milled. The timber was cut high in the nearby Sierra Nevada, sent down to the lake in flumes, and floated to the mills.

"There are so many people on this road and in the valley here, that we won't have any trouble," one of the deputies commented as they prepared for the final leg of their journey.

"It'll be dark by the time we get to Lakeview," the other deputy said, with the driver nodding agreement. "If someone is going to try something, that's where it will be. There's lots of timber, lots of big rock formations, and not much traffic after dark."

The trip around Washoe Lake and across the long valley went without mishap, and they were several miles from climbing out of the valley at Lakeview when the sun went down. It was a moonless night, but the road was so well used that staying on the road wasn't difficult. The two deputies closed up and rode close to the wagon, constantly looking out just as far as their eyes would let them.

***

"According to the wire, Spencer left Reno well before ten this morning, Jacob," Hawkeye Byrnes said. "He's coming on a wagon escorted by two Washoe County deputies. That's not the way I'd handle it."

"Yeah," Chance snarled. "A platoon of deputies, maybe, but sure as hell more than two."

A couple of days before, when Chance jumped at the idea of working as lead investigator for the attorney general, he had a long talk with Byrnes about what kind of life he was looking for. "I love this position in Virginia City, but very truthfully, I want much more, and I want it to be in law enforcement.

"Like many, I guess, I've thought about bounty hunting, but so many bounty hunters I've run into are almost criminals themselves, I don't think I'd be very good at it. Being a local sheriff or town marshal is okay for the older men, but I want to be very active."

Chance listened to the man, reflecting on his own background, how he had whipped a bad man and was instantly a sheriff in a small town and how that grew fast into being a part of the Marshal Service. *Hawkeye's still almost a boy, but I can see him as a deputy in the service.*

"I'm going to ask you to do something for me, Byrnes. Take a leave of absence from your positions in Virginia City and come to work for me as an investigator with the attorney general's office. If it works out like I think it will, I'll ask Ira Stone to pull a couple of his strong strings, and get you appointed to the Marshal Service."

Hawkeye Byrnes seemed to grow three inches when Chance said that, his eyes lit up like beacons in the night, and he gave a rebel yell that rocked the old courthouse high on B Street on the Comstock. Chance snickered. "I take that as a yes."

Now, Chance wondered why the Washoe County sheriff would only send two deputies to guard Spencer. "If you were going to kill Spencer, where would you take him out?" Chance had gone over the maps of the road between Reno and Carson City and knew where he would make the hit, and wanted to see what Byrnes had in mind. "After all, you sure recognized the spot Dougherty was using to try to take out Stanfield."

"I've made that ride many times, Chance," Byrnes said. "It's well traveled, lots of people on horseback, in buggies, and many wagons moving everything under the sun back and forth. The road narrows considerably at Lakeview, there's lots of timber and big boulders, and based on when that wagon left Reno, they would be at Lakeview well after sundown. If there's a hit planned, that's where it will happen."

"Let's take a ride, Hawkeye. Bring a heavy jacket and good gloves, and make sure you have your rifle. We're gonna set up a hawk's nest for Mr. Hawkeye Byrnes." He laughed, grabbing that big bearskin coat and floppy sombrero.

"Let's see if we can find a good spot to shoot Spencer and then find a good spot to shoot the shooter. I doubt the shooter would get there this early so we have the advantage, Mr. Byrnes. Never forget the pleasure of having the advantage."

***

Monty Smith got the word from one of Sheriff Doyle's deputies that Spencer would be brought to Carson City on a wagon, and the deputy even told him what time the wagon would be leaving Reno. Smith was a regular at the Silver Star and had become a friend with Deputy Olsen. Olsen would never have imagined that Smith, who he thought was simply a working cowboy, was a paid gunman, looking to kill Spencer.

Smith was deadly with his rifle and the original job had been to kill Stanfield, but with the revelations of Spencer's secretary, Seamus O'Brien made some fast adjustments. "You kill Spencer first, and then we'll talk about Stanfield again." Smith could see two paychecks coming his way instead of just one.

"Be cold out there once that sun goes down," Smith commented. "You and the other deputies going to be on hand to escort Spencer into Carson City?"

"Nah," Olsen laughed, "that'd be a waste of time. Sheriff likes us to be right in town, where the action is."

Thirty miles would put that wagon north of Lakeview when the sun goes down, Smith reasoned. *I can get out there before the sun goes down and be ready for Mr. Spencer. He's sure to have a guard or two, but I can scatter them after shooting Spencer.*

In his talks with Deputy Olsen and while setting up the hit with Seamus O'Brien, nothing had been said about how Sean Dougherty had been shot to death just before he readied himself to kill Stanfield. Smith might not have been quite so sure of himself if he knew.

Smith had a heavy buffalo robe tied to the back of his saddle and counted on more than one person seeing him ride out of town, toward the east. He mentioned a couple of times at the Silver Star that he was going to Dayton to meet a charming young lady. He did ride east for a couple of miles before turning back north and skirting along the base of the mountains, toward Lakeview.

He spent less than half an hour scouting for a good shooting position, tethered his horse in a stand of piñon pines, and crept up to a rocky point about two hundred yards from the road. *My old Henry will have a one-sided conversation with Mr. Spencer*, he thought, pulling that heavy robe around his shoulders. It was just getting dusk and he figured it would be at least an hour before the wagon and outriders arrived.

There are several ranches in the area, and the road through the Franktown area, climbing to the gap in the mountains known as Lakeview, had less and less traffic as the day wore on. Flumes that carried water down from the Sierra Nevada on the west and up and over the top of the Virginia Range to Virginia City interrupted the scenery some, but the road itself stood out in plain view.

***

"That's where I'd bed down," Hawkeye Byrnes said, pointing to a rocky cliff that overlooked the road that climbed out of Washoe Valley. "A man using a good rifle would have a clean shot at someone in a buggy or wagon."

"You're right on that," Chance said, scanning the area. "He'd be out of sight from down below, be able to steady the rifle, and be a good marksman. What do you know about this cowboy named Monty Smith?"

"He worked in Texas after the war, but not as a cowboy. His gun was for rent on either side of any question that might be asked. What brought him to Nevada and Orion Seamus O'Brien's ranch, I don't know. He's quarrelsome, likes his liquor, and has no respect for women."

"You seem to know quite a bit about the man," Chance muttered.

"He spent some time in Virginia City and I made it a point to suggest that he might find a better climate some south of town." Byrnes chuckled. "We need to hang our hats someplace where we can see him plain as anything and still be able to nab him if he tries to skedaddle. Someplace like those trees right over there," he said, pointing to a stand of pines.

"Well," Chance drawled out slow, "no, not there. Now, Hawkeye, picture you coming up here to kill a man, where would you tie your horse?"

"Oh, my. Maybe we hadn't ought to bed down where he'd put that horse, now. No siree, that wouldn't be the place. We do want to be above him, though."

The two lawmen spent another half hour finding just the place, got their horses tied off and out of sight, and got settled in. Chance found a telescope in one of his pockets, and searched around the area. "Nice little buck right down there, if we get hungry." He grinned, pointing down into a meadow half a mile away.

Chapter Ten

"That sun sure does go down early this time of year, don't it?" Donny Sheridan said, riding alongside the wagon. "It's gonna be one cold ride into Carson City. I ain't ridin' back tonight. Sheriff can just wait 'till tomorrow to see me."

Bones Johnson the wagon driver just snorted, spit some juice out the side, and ignored the deputy. Sheridan rode on forward to where his partner Stan Fields rode. "Cold," he said.

"Get the hell back where you belong," Fields snapped. "Comin' dark, dammit. You just left the rear of that wagon unguarded, now get back there." Sheridan tightened up and wanted to tell Fields to ride back there himself, but didn't.

"Who made you the boss?" Sheridan snapped. "Ain't nobody back there and won't be. This whole thing is a waste of our time. I'm gonna hit a saloon as soon as we drop this Spencer guy off. I hate the cold."

"You're gonna hate it worse when you're out of a job, Sheridan. I've got you ranked and I've got the desire to be boss, so get back there now." Fields had been bucking for a big promotion for some time, and getting Sheridan fired over something like ignoring security would sure be a good thing.

As they climbed through the heavy timber along the west side of Washoe Valley, past the ranches tucked away off the road, it got dark as dark can get. "Get out of these trees in a mile or so and we'll at least be able to see the road," Fields murmured. "Sheriff was wrong just sending the two of us, and very wrong sending Sheridan, and I'm the one be telling him," and he smiled at that thought.

***

Chance nudged Byrnes and pointed down toward the rock outcrop below them, motioning to be quiet. Byrnes watched Monty Smith ride into the stand of pines and tie off his horse. He didn't try to hide or be quiet, just sauntered across the face of the hill and tucked himself into position. Byrnes snickered watching Smith pull a flask and take a long drink. *Sure hope that's whiskey he's guzzling,* he thought. *Sure glad we didn't tie our horses in those trees.* He almost nodded a thank you at Chance.

Chance had the telescope up, looking down the road and around into the valley below. "They're about two miles out," he whispered. "Made very good time. You keep your rifle trained on Smith and I'll keep you informed as to where the wagon is."

Byrnes had the rifle resting comfortably in the crook of his arm and had an excellent view of Smith's back. "Remember," Chance whispered, "we don't want Spencer killed. We want that man alive. When Smith brings his rifle to bear, you shoot. It's best if we don't kill him, either."

The lead deputy came into view and the wagon came up shortly. Smith eased his rifle into position, pulled it tight into his shoulder, and Hawkeye Byrnes watched him thumb back the hammer. Byrnes sighted on Smith's left arm, cradling the rifle, and slowly squeezed off a round, blowing Smith's elbow into several pieces.

The reaction caused Smith to fire his big Henry, but the bullet never got within ten yards of anyone in, on, or near the wagon. Fields turned his horse and motioned for Bones Johnson to put those horses into a full gallop and rode alongside. He looked around for Sheridan, but the deputy was nowhere in sight. Sheridan had stopped some time back to relieve himself and when he heard the shot he was well over half a mile behind the wagon.

Fields was busy getting that wagon moving as fast as it would go, trying to find Sheridan, and never saw the two lawmen as they loped down the mountainside and took one Monty Smith into custody. "Nasty little cut there, Mr. Smith," Byrnes said, ripping the man's shirtsleeve off and using it to stem some serious bleeding. "Fall down, or something?"

Chance brought the horses up and they got the handcuffed Smith into the saddle for the short ride into Carson City. It was an easy jaunt across the side of the hill to get on the main road and they were riding down Carson Street within the hour. "Sheriff Doyle, I'm Inspector Chance and this is my deputy, Hawkeye Byrnes. We need to book this man into your jail for attempted murder.

"You might want to call a doctor, too, if you have a mind to, he's hurtin' some."

"Glad to meet you, Chance. Heard you went to work for Barlow. Jail's filling up tonight. They just brought Spencer in from Reno. Said there was some trouble near Lakeview but didn't know if it had been aimed at them."

"It was, and this is the trouble. Keep a good close eye on them, sheriff. I'll be back in the morning with all the paperwork for both men."

Chance nodded to Byrnes and the two walked out. "They have some nice steaks at the St. Charles, Mr. Byrnes. Care to join me?"

It took just minutes to walk to the hotel and find a table at the restaurant and order supper. "We need to change our tactics, Hawkeye. So far we have been responding to their thrusts, and it's time to take a more aggressive approach to our problem. There is more than one person behind these attempts on Judge Stanfield's life and we need to track them down."

"Somebody has been paying for all this," Byrnes said, shaking his head in agreement with Chance.

"That's right, and I think we have a good chance of catching 'em up. According to Ira Stone, money has also been flowing into the pockets of some of the legislators who will be meeting in just a couple of weeks, right across the street there. What I see, and what we have to stop, is, if Judge Stanfield is out of the way, his majority opinion won't be written before the legislature meets, and then, those legislators being paid big money will write a water law favorable to our conspirators. You and I are the only ones who can stop that from happening."

Hawkeye sat back in his chair, letting the full impact of that fall into place. "That's just about a big responsibility, marshal. What's our first move?"

Chance liked that there was no hesitation in the young man, that he recognized the size of the problem and was ready to jump in, with both feet in the stirrups. "We need to spend some time with Smith and Spencer, and I think I know how to get the truth from them. I'll interview Spencer while you interview Smith. Then we'll write up what we learned, and switch around. I'll interview Smith and you interview Spencer.

"Without indicating that we know what each said to the other of us, we might get them in either a big lie or get some good names. Let's meet first thing in the morning and make our plans.

"Because of the information from Ted Whistler, we know many of the names already, and we know how much money has been filtered into the politicians. There's no reason to believe that others would be paying for the gunmen. We'll concentrate on those ranchers whose names we know." Chance saw agreement in Hawkeye Byrnes' face and felt certain that they would bring this conspiracy to a close soon.

"We'll take the fight to them for a change," Chance said. "We may or may not have enough evidence for Barlow to issue arrest warrants, but some strong questioning of these arrogant ranchers might help some. Hired gunmen make me want to puke, Hawkeye. It's bad enough to kill a man, but it's a coward that hires that killing, and I don't like cowards."

They finished their supper with pie and coffee and went their separate ways, looking forward to getting to the bottom of the conspiracy to take out the judge. Hawkeye had taken a room above a furniture shop just a block behind the Silver Star Saloon, and he stopped in for an after-supper brandy on the way home.

"Sheriff Hawkeye Byrnes," the barman said. "We don't see you down off that big old mountain of silver very often, and surely not late at night. What can I get you?" Seth Blanchard had worked several saloons on the Comstock and had moved down to Carson City just recently.

"You look as comfortable here as you always did at the Washoe Club, Seth. I'm working for the attorney general now, so you just might see me a bit more often. I'm sure you can find some good brandy tucked away back there, eh?"

"Coming right up, Hawkeye. The attorney general, huh? Hear tell he's a real stickler for following the law."

"Indeed, Seth, indeed." Hawkeye Byrnes spent an hour sipping some good brandy and talking with Seth Blanchard, watching some of the early night action at the gambling tables, and was starting to call it a night when Deputy Gerald Olsen walked in.

"Gimme a beer, Seth. What a night and it's just starting," Olsen said, almost nudging Byrnes as he stepped up to the bar. "Damn marshals and special investigators got all of us hopping."

Byrnes gave a quick little nod to Seth and kept quiet himself. *This might just be a little bit of fun*, he thought with a wry grin.

"Damn Virginia City sheriff's working for that retired marshal and both of them are working for Elmer Barlow, and everybody thinks they can just waltz into our offices and give out orders. That sheriff shot Dougherty dead the other morning, and then, sure as hell, he shot old Monty Smith earlier this evening, and he and Marshal Chance just pop in and give us a body or a shot up cowboy. Damn fools," Olsen snapped, downing more than half his pint in one swallow.

Byrnes snickered, motioning Seth Ballard for another brandy. "What are you laughin' at?" Olsen demanded, slamming his empty glass on the bar.

"Take it easy, deputy," Byrnes said with a smile. "You always drink on the job and in uniform?"

"None of your damn business," Olsen snarled, turning to face Byrnes, letting his hand snake down toward his holster. "Who you think you are, questioning a lawman? I'm the lawman in this town, you got that?" The threat was very obvious and Seth Ballard stepped back a few feet knowing that Byrnes was much faster, meaner, and deadlier than Olsen could ever be.

"Take it easy, Deputy Olsen," Byrnes said, both his hands spread gently on the top of the bar. "My name is Hawkeye Byrnes, special investigator for Attorney General Elmer Barstow, and one of those damn fools who bring you prisoners and bodies of bad guys. Still want to make a play?"

Olsen's face fell, his eyes went blank, he backed away two steps, stared long into the flint-steel eyes of Byrnes, turned, and walked quickly out of the saloon. "Man has a hard time making conversation, eh Seth? Well, one more little brandy and I'll go home and quit making problems for you." He laughed. Seth was trying to chuckle pouring that one last brandy.

Olsen will never know just how close to dying he was tonight, Ballard understood.

***

Orion Seamus O'Brien was sitting in a large leather armchair in front of a blazing fire in his living room. Mounted deer, antelope, and elk heads adorned walls of rough-hewn timber, steer and bear hides were stretched and hung, and a massive buffalo head was mounted directly over the fireplace. Some intense banging on the front door interrupted an after-supper glass of good Irish whiskey.

He flung the door open and found Nate Burleson and Henry Carrington. "Nate, Henry," O'Brien said. "My goodness, what's this?"

"Your Mr. Smith is in jail and Spencer is very much alive and well, Seamus," Carrington snarled, stepping quickly into the warmth of the ranch house. "Marshal Chance and his assistant, Phineas Byrnes, wounded Smith and allowed the Washoe deputies to bring Spencer to the capital.

"This is getting more and more out of control. We've forgotten the immense power that our money has and given way to an abuse of violence. It has backfired on us. We will have that damned retired marshal at our throats before the legislature meets."

O'Brien poured whiskies around and the men settled into leather chairs near the roaring fire, contemplating the situation. "I only know one way to get that Marshal Chance to back off," the big Irish rancher said.

"If you're talking murder, again, I'm not going to back you," Carrington said. "He's the chief investigator for the attorney general right now, is a retired U.S. marshal, and has the deck of cards stacked in his favor all the way."

"No," O'Brien said, "I'm not talking killing the man," a slight grin showing across his ruddy face. "His family, his wife and two children, will be joining him in Carson City sometime next week, according to a rumor I heard. If we had them in our possession, he would gladly convince that judge not to finish his majority opinion before the legislature opens their session."

It was very quiet in that large living room, and O'Brien slowly got up, threw a couple of logs on the fire, and replenished each of the glasses with fresh whiskey. Furtive glances were made, there was a cough or two, and no one spoke for more than a full minute.

"No!" Carrington said. "I can't support that, and I won't. I won't support more killing either."

"If we don't do something, we will not just lose the water fight, we'll probably end up in prison," O'Brien said. "This would give us a chance."

Nate Burleson stood up and paced a couple of times back and forth in front of the fireplace, took a long drink of whiskey, and finally said, "I was behind the attempted stagecoach attack on the judge, have spent considerable money buying legislative votes, and helped pay for Smith's abortive attack on Spencer.

"Right now, Spencer, Smith, Johnny Ferris, and Sonny Lauck are in jail and you can bet Chance will have our names within the next day or two. We can't wait a week, gentlemen. We can't wait for Chance's family to come to us. We either must kill Chance and the judge in the next two days, or we must leave in the morning for Preston and abduct his family."

He was interrupted by Carrington. "Nonsense," he snarled, jumping to his feet. "It's over, you fools. It's time to work on making the consequences as small as possible. That marshal will have our names tomorrow. We need to figure out how to make our jail terms as short as possible."

The reality of the situation was still not fully understood by O'Brien, but Burleson nodded his head in agreement. "Carrington is right," he almost whispered. "There may be one out for us, though. Smith knows us and Spencer knows us. Lauck and Ferris don't. Would it be possible to do away with Smith and Spencer, in that Carson

City Jail? It wouldn't solve our water law problem, but it would keep that marshal from knowing our names.

"We've lost the water law, I'm afraid, but there's still a chance that we can keep from going to prison." Burleson could see defeat in Carrington's eyes, could feel it in himself, but only saw anger and bitterness in O'Brien's face. "What are you thinking, Seamus?" he asked.

"I don't go down without fighting all the way to the ground, Nate, as you well know. I have a thousand acres of good grass, several hundred head of fine cattle, sheep roaming the hills around us, and a fine home that I built myself, and I'm not willing to roll over and give it all up.

"I agree, we've run out of time as far as the water law problem goes. There simply isn't enough time to take Chance's family before he gets our names. I don't think there's a gunman left in Nevada who could take out Chance and Byrnes, and that just about leaves us with that one option, kill Spencer and Smith."

"I've listened to both of you," Carrington said, "dejected and beaten, and I have to agree. I'm not willing to let my ranch go over this, I'm not the kind of man that would do well in prison, but I'm not the least bit sure we're going to be able to kill Spencer and Smith tomorrow or the next day."

"It's for sure we can't hire someone," O'Brien said, almost with a snicker. "We don't seem to be very good at that. I say we simply blow up the damn jail. Dynamite is available by the ton because of the mines, I worked as a powder monkey underground, that's how I made enough money to get my ranch started." He sat back in his big, comfortable chair and smiled for the first time since Carrington and Burleson arrived.

"If we leave in the next hour or so, we can be at that jail while it's still dark, plant our charges, and blow that building to pieces. I use dynamite a lot, blasting out tree stumps and big rocks in the pastures. All of us do. I've got plenty enough and caps and fuse, to take out that puny little jail."

He stood up and poured each of them another glass of whiskey, and raised his glass in a toast. "To the demise of Spencer and Smith, and to the continued success of our ranches and lives," he said, taking his glass down in one swallow. Burleson and Carrington joined in the toast.

The three ranchers didn't seem to understand the importance of the papers that had been turned over to Marshal Chance by Ted Whistler. Names, dates, and amounts paid to legislators. Names, dates, and amounts set aside for finding men to kill Supreme Court Justice Amos Stanfield. Those papers were in the possession of the Nevada attorney general who was contemplating issuing arrest warrants for every name mentioned. At least those still left alive.

Chapter Eleven

It was nearing four in the morning as the three riders slipped into Carson City. The saddle bags on O'Brien's horse were stuffed with sticks of dynamite and burn fuse, and Burleson's saddle carried a box of blasting caps and tape. "The cells are along the east wall, I think," Carrington said. "Those walls are made of stone, so the blast should be deadly."

They dismounted about half a block from the jail, noticed that there was the slightest light coming from inside the offices, and worked around behind the structure. "We'll want to get the dynamite well under this rock," O'Brien said, trying to be quiet moving dirt from around the base of the wall. "Damn rock goes down two feet or more," he snarled.

They didn't have time to dig down two feet, and simply taped several sticks together to make up a package, and placed at least four packages as close to the walls as possible, covering them back up with what was dug up. They had measured their burn cord so the blasts would be sequential, about five minutes from when the fuses were lit.

"Did you measure them right?" O'Brien asked. "You get about forty-five seconds to a foot, remember." He lit a match and got the four fuses lit and they walked back, mounted up, and were well away from the jail when the blasts went off.

The ground shook, windows rattled for half a mile around, and many residents were seen in their nightshirts coming out to see what the commotion was all about. Every dog in Carson City was howling and barking, and men were heard yelling for the fire brigades.

O'Brien had a smile on his face when he and Burleson tethered their horses near the Silver Star Saloon. Carrington said he wouldn't be going in, and rode for his ranch. Half a mile out of town, he stopped and emptied his stomach, and stopped two more times, before he reached home. *All we had to do was buy that old fool, and now I'm a wanted man for murder. What have I allowed myself to become? If Irene had lived she would hate me for what I've done. I know I have to run, but where? Where would I go?*

O'Brien and Burleson were standing at the bar in the almost empty saloon and watched the sun bounce light off the U.S. Mint across the street. They could hear the fire bells ringing, watched men and horses run toward the sheriff's jailhouse, and sipped good whiskey.

"You boys are out and about mighty early," Ned Twimble, the late night, early morning barman said. "Wonder who was doing the blasting this early?"

"Whoever, they'll catch hell for doing it this early," Seamus O'Brien laughed. "Must have got away from 'em, though," he mused. "Lots of fire laddies moving. Hope nobody got themselves hurt."

Burleson stifled a chuckle by taking a swig of whiskey and watched another horse-drawn hose cart dash down Telegraph Street. "Maybe I'll take a wander over and see what the action is," he said. "I enjoy watching the fire boys do their work. Never have wanted to, myself."

"I'm heading back to the ranch," O'Brien said. "Did enough blasting when I worked the Aurora district. Swing by later, Nate," he said, quaffing the last of his whiskey and heading for the door. Burleson walked down the sidewalk toward where the fire wagons were moving.

***

"Who the hell would be blasting this time of the morning?" Jacob Chance said, sliding out of bed in his second-floor hotel room. "Damn fools." Following the multiple blasts he heard the fire bells clanging, then the noise of the fire laddies trying to get the hose carts and hand pumpers moving and decided to dress and find the action. The desk clerk called him over and said it was the jail, that someone had blown it up.

Chance ran the three blocks to the sheriff's jail and offices only to find chaos. Only the night duty deputy had been in the offices and he was badly injured and taken to the hospital, and there was no one to tell him about the prisoners. Chance had faced situations like this in the past and assumed command.

The attorney general had given him a badge and he pinned it on, and found the man who commanded the fire brigades. "I'm Inspector Chance of the attorney general's office. The sheriff isn't around, and I'm taking charge. Where are the prisoners?"

"The cells were along that wall there," the chief said, "the one that isn't there anymore. We have found three people dead, one barely alive, and don't know if there were any others."

"Where are they now?" Chance asked, and the chief pointed to some trees in the front yard of a residence near the jail. "If you find any others, get them over there too. I wonder where the sheriff is?"

"Home sleeping," the chief laughed. Chance walked to the yard and found Spencer's body laid out, severely mangled from the explosion. Ferris's body was nearby, and one other that he couldn't identify. It took him a couple of minutes to find Monty Smith, sitting up under a tree, nursing some bad cuts to his head and body from flying stone and steel.

"He isn't going anywhere," Chance muttered, and then spotted Sammy Lauck being attended to by a couple of local ladies. "At least I know where my prisoners are," he said. Within a couple of minutes he found two deputies coming to the scene and brought them up to date. About that time Hawkeye Byrnes came running up.

"Did we lose them all?" he asked, not even breathing hard from his five-block run. Chance questioned that and Byrnes answered simply, "Virginia City is more than six thousand feet above sea level, marshal. Running at this lower altitude down here, hell, I've got more oxygen than I'm used to. Besides, I like to run."

"I always figured that getting there fast is why we have horses," Chance snorted, remembering how hard he was breathing when he came panting in that morning. *The good life at the ranch is killing me,* he thought with a smile.

"Spencer and Ferris are dead but Smith and Lauck are still alive. We might still get some names, if we're lucky. Smith will probably tell us that Spencer hired him and Lauck about the same, but we gotta try."

"When they're all busted up like this would be a good time to start," Byrnes said. "They won't be thinking straight."

"Good idea," Chance said. "You take Smith, remind him it was you who shot him,"—he snickered—"and I'll take Mr. Lauck. Pin your badge on, Hawkeye. These town people don't know us and might get pushy if we start pestering the prisoners." Chance walked over to where the women were treating Lauck's wounds and introduced himself.

"This man was a prisoner in the jail, so I need to ask him some questions. You can keep right on working on him, if you need to." He smiled at one of the ladies.

"I've heard of you, Marshal Chance," the matronly lady said. "No, I don't want anything to do with this vile man. He used foul language when we tried to help him, and threatened poor Mrs. Kennedy something awful. No, marshal, he's all yours, and maybe you could teach him some manners." She snickered, almost flirting just a bit.

"I might just do that, ma'am." He smiled. "Thank you. Now, Mr. Lauck, we meet again, eh? Ferris is dead and so is Spencer, and what that means is, all of the problems that the three of you faced are yours alone, now. You have a chance to help yourself, though. Tell me who was paying you to set up that hit on the judge and I'm in a position to lower the charges against you."

"Shove it somewhere, marshal. I ain't tellin' you nothin'. What are you talkin' about anyway?" he asked. "Nobody was payin' me nothin'."

"The argument at the Sazerac Saloon was about how the money wasn't going to be paid because Spencer ran away. Who was paying it, and why did Spencer run away," Chance snarled, and pushed Lauck just enough that all the wounds hurt all at the same time.

He cried out, startling the women, and the one piped up, "Teach him again, marshal." Chance snickered, jabbed Lauck gently, and demanded an answer.

"Spencer offered me money to set up a hit, then withdrew the offer," Lauck said, almost whimpering. One of the deputies came over when Chance motioned to him.

"Better get him to the hospital, and keep him in restraints. The attorney general has an indefinite hold on this man, and the one over there." He pointed to where Byrnes was talking to Smith.

Chance walked over and knelt down next to Byrnes. "Good morning, Mr. Smith. You have all the luck, eh? First Mr. Byrnes here shoots you, then the people that paid you try to blow you up. You seem to be in everyone's sights." He looked over at Byrnes and stood up. "Anything?"

"I think so. He works for one of the ranchers, a man named Orion O'Brien, and following a meeting with other ranchers in the Carson Valley, they offered him a good sum of money to knock off Spencer. He said he doesn't even know Spencer, but the ranchers feared what Spencer might tell you. They mentioned your name often in their discussion."

"Did he happen to mention the name Nate Burleson?"

"Yup, that was one of them, and the other was Henry Carrington."

"Now we're getting somewhere, Hawkeye Byrnes. Burleson has been behind the effort to assassinate Judge Stanfield all along, using Spencer as his go-between. I want you to stick like glue to Mr. Smith until he is safe in a cell somewhere. I'm going to spread the word that all the prisoners were killed, but that might not be enough. They will go after Smith with everything they have, Byrnes, so you keep him safe."

"Do you see the feller in the frock coat and black hat by the white fence over there?" Chance nodded *yes* and Byrnes continued. "When I was talking with Smith, he kept looking over at the man, angry like. I'd bet he is one of the ranchers and Smith believes they tried to kill him with that blast."

"I believe that, too." Chance chuckled. "I'll check him out, Byrnes. Get this feller some medical help and see if you can find him a cell in the Carson City Prison for a few days. Meet me at the hotel for lunch if we don't run into each other before that."

Chance found one of the deputies trying to save some of the department paper work and pointed out the man in the frock coat. "He's a rancher south of here, in the Carson Valley. Name's Burleson, I think, Nathaniel Burleson. I just saw him leave the Silver Star with another rancher, O'Brien, when I was on my way here. What a mess," he said, trying to work through several tons of blasted rock walls.

Chance nodded his thanks and walked back uptown and into the Silver Star Saloon. *I can't seem to get it out of my head that the sheriff didn't bother to show up. He either lives a long way out of town or,* and he paused in his thoughts, *maybe he knew that something like this was in the works. I really don't want to find that to be true.*

"Morning," he said, as he walked in, making sure the AG badge could be seen. It was just after sunrise and the bar was full. "Looks like everyone in town got woke up early, eh?" he said to the bartender. "Got any coffee back there?"

"Been a run on coffee." Ned Trimble laughed. "Most want a bit of something else along with it. You too?"

"Nope, just coffee is fine for me. Seen Nate Burleson this morning?"

"Are you that U.S. marshal that's here because of threats to old Judge Stanfield? Sure wouldn't want anything bad to happen to that gentleman. And, to answer your question,"–he snickered–"Burleson and O'Brien came in just before the blast and left right after."

Chance took a good sip of some strong coffee and smiled his thanks to the bartender. "I don't want anything to happen to that judge either. Name's Chance, Jacob Chance, and yes, I was a marshal, now I have a nice ranch down Preston way. Those ranchers come in early like that often?"

"No, that's kinda rare. Probly some kind of meetin' or something. I think the whole town's up this morning, though. Here, have some more coffee, get your blood warmed up.

"This is the way it is during the legislature, only instead of them coming in early, they're staying late." Trimble cackled, getting a good laugh from Chance, too. "You keep that old judge safe, marshal," he said, and moved down the bar to spread more joy and wisdom. *That is my plan,* Chance said to himself.

***

Hawkeye Byrnes helped get Smith to the hospital, stayed right with him while the doctors patched him up, and then, with some help from a couple of deputies, took the man to the Carson City Prison, on the eastern outskirts of the city. Smith and Byrnes were in the back of a wagon being driven by one of the deputies. Another deputy rode along behind. Byrnes' horse was tied to the back of the wagon.

"This will be a bumpy ride, Smith, but it can't be helped. So, first O'Brien pays you to kill Spencer and then turns around and tries to blow you up when you got caught. Don't need to work for a man like that." Byrnes was doing his best to become Smith's best friend and get as much information as he could from the man.

"Why did they want Spencer dead? Wasn't he an attorney?"

"Yeah, but before too many people found out about it, he was the man that handled the money and made the deals that O'Brien and Burleson wanted done. They figured since he got caught that he'd tell all about that. Bastards tried to kill me too, I guess, and you're damn right, I'm telling you."

Byrnes remembered the sheaf of papers that Chance showed him in his old office in Virginia City, the ones Whistler had given him, outlining how the ranchers got things done by way of Spencer. *Now, we have one of the men actually paid by one of the ranchers. That makes those Whistler papers even more valuable.*

It was a good ride from the hospital to the state prison in an area called Warm Springs, between the city proper and the Carson River. "I'm gonna set you up in the prison, Smith. That way you'll be pretty safe, and if you'll testify against these guys that are trying to kill you, I think we can get you a good deal with a judge." Smith actually knew he would be safe in the prison, and figured it would be better than the city jail had been.

"Here's the deal, Smith," Byrnes said. "Attempted murder on a prisoner carries a pretty hefty prison sentence, but, if you continue to work with me, we can ease that off quite a bit." Smith kept right on agreeing with whatever Byrnes asked, still talking as they rode through the big gates and into the impressive state prison.

"I'm Special Investigator Byrnes with the attorney general's office, and I need accommodations for this gentleman until they can get that jail rebuilt," he told the warden.

"Heard the blast clear out here." Warden Wayne Courson chuckled. "Everybody dead? Well, I guess not, looking at this fellow. What happened?"

"I think some people wanted to keep this man quiet and maybe a couple of others. At least three prisoners died, but we need to keep this one alive and away from other people. He needs to be alone."

"We can take care of that," Courson said. "Peters, put him in solitary, but don't rough him up any more than that explosion's already done. Get him fed and some new clothes. Remember, he isn't a prisoner yet, just a guest." He chuckled.

"Come on in, Byrnes, and fill out some paperwork. I thought you were the sheriff up on the Comstock. When'd you go to work for old Barlow?"

"Seems as though a lot of people want to kill Judge Stanfield, and Marshal Chance and I are gonna keep that from happening," he said. Courson offered coffee and the two chatted for a while.

"That's a nasty business, killing a judge. Seems to me that too many people seem to think they can just take whatever they want with no consequences to others. It ain't right to take all the water from a river just because it's there. Other people need that water too. That's what old Stanfield is working on. Burleson and his gang are simply greedy and selfish, and 'cause they have some money, think they can do anything they want." Warden Courson was on a soapbox, Byrnes thought, but was sure right in his thoughts.

"If we're lucky, warden, me and Chance will be bringing you some new guests soon. There've been a hundred or more laws broke so far." He chuckled. "Keep Mr. Smith alive and well for me. I'll be back to talk with him some more."

"I'll do that, Byrnes, and if you get a chance, bring that marshal by, I'd like to meet him."

Chapter Twelve

Byrnes checked out the damaged jail scene after leaving the prison, and found Sheriff Micah Doyle pacing around and grumbling. "Morning, sheriff," Byrnes said. "Was there anything left of the blasting agents that were used? Sure could use some real evidence on this little episode."

There was complete devastation, as if two sides in a war clashed on this very spot, using artillery barrages at will. Rather than a rock wall, Byrnes saw a field of gravel and wondered how anyone had survived such a blast. They must have used at least twice the amount of dynamite that was necessary, he contemplated, and wondered again where the sheriff had been and what took him so long to respond.

"Hello, Byrnes. What the hell do you care about evidence? This isn't a Virginia City crime, it's a Carson City crime. None of your business."

"Whoa up there, Doyle, don't get yourself in a twit. You're already aware that I'm an investigator for the Nevada attorney general, and those were our prisoners that were attacked, some of whom were flat out killed. Now, did you find any explosive leftovers that we could use?"

"To hell with the attorney general, it was my jail that got blown up. Go look for any evidence yourself." His shoulders were slumped in utter defeat, Byrnes noted, and he wondered just when it was he finally showed up. He wandered through the rubble field, noting by way of blasted out holes in the ground where each bundle of dynamite had been placed. He had a good idea of how the charges were laid in but wondered just how he and Chance would be able to pin the explosion on any particular person or group.

We know who is responsible for this, but how in the name of Texas Almighty are we gonna prove it? He was almost laughing at his own comments, and thought again about what Chance had said about those that hired someone to kill another. "I wonder if they hired somebody to do this or if they discovered gajones and did it themselves? If they hired someone to do this, we have a whole new problem to face. Will Stanfield's home be the next to explode?"

After spending more than an hour going through the rubble, he had a small amount of material in his saddlebags and rode the few blocks uptown to have lunch with Chance. "Simple sticks of dynamite, which is pretty easy to come by, regular blasting caps, and they used burn fuse." He was holding a pretty good conversation with himself as he tied off near the St. Charles Hotel. "I wonder why they used so much dynamite?" He smiled. "The plan wasn't to break those men out of prison, they wanted those men dead."

He was still shaking his head as he walked into the hotel and into the restaurant, spotting Chance across the room and joining him. "Looks like the sheriff is in a fine twit, Chance," Byrnes said, pulling up a chair and joining the marshal. "He bit my head off, but I set him straight about whose jurisdiction this crime was in. Smith is in the state prison, and he gave me most of the details about his attempted hit on Spencer."

Byrnes got himself settled in and broke the bad news to Chance. "If our rancher friends hired someone to blow up that jail, we may have a problem. Do you think Stanfield would stand to be relocated? An unknown bomber scares the hell out of me."

"You've been busy, Hawkeye. That was Burleson you spotted near the jail and he and O'Brien had been seen in town just before the blast, and then had drinks at the Silver Spur after the blast, so we have enough to make me want to take a ride to one or more ranches today.

"I think we might have a chat with the judge about such a move, but I can almost hear his words. 'They ain't gonna chase me out of my own home.' No, we'll talk to him, but he would never go for it. We'll let Augie Roark know our concerns, too," he said.

"There's a third man, a Henry Carrington, involved, according to Smith. Smith worked for O'Brien and there was a meeting of all three ranchers when they hired him to kill Spencer. Carrington kept arguing against the plan, but finally went along with the other two. All three coughed up the money they paid Smith." He took a sip of coffee, and continued.

"Seems that Spencer is the one that did most of the hiring and spreading the plans that were to be used. Burleson and O'Brien provided the money and most of the plans, and they wanted him dead because of how much he knew. Smith said that Carrington was the one that believed in buying people, not killing them. He feels that Stanfield should have been bought, like the legislators, not killed."

"That's pretty much what we got from Whistler, and Smith backs it up nicely. All the names are falling into place. Good work, Hawkeye," Chance said.

"I went over the blast scene pretty close and those boys used a lot of explosives. I thought the plan was an attempted breakout, but I'm sure now that they were definitely trying to kill whoever was in those cells. That jail was disintegrated, Chance, and how Smith lived through it is a miracle."

"Burleson and O'Brien were right about not being able to buy their way out of the water deal, Byrnes," Chance said. "Amos Stanfield could never be bought. And you're right about the blast designed to kill, not free, the prisoners.

"Let's plan a meeting with the AG for this afternoon and then, based on what comes out of that, visit some ranchers tomorrow. We may have enough evidence that he might want to issue some warrants.

"What's your opinion of Sheriff Doyle? Is he simply slow, or doesn't give a damn, or is he part of the conspiracy?"

"He's a politician first, not a lawman, so I wouldn't call him slow, but I'll certainly go along with the idea that he doesn't give a damn. He took the job of sheriff to move toward the legislature, and possibly the governor's mansion, if they ever get it built." Byrnes snickered. "We're sure that many in the legislature have been bought, as far as this water law situation is concerned, and it wouldn't surprise me if some money found its way into Doyle's pockets. Enough for him to ignore certain happenings and such.

"Between Burleson and O'Brien, there is one hell of a lot of money that could be in play on this table. Burleson has ties to the timber interests in the high mountains as well, and they supply the timber for the mines. Between ranching money, timber money and mining money, you could buy just about anything you ever thought of."

"Ralston and his Bank of California have control of many Comstock mines, all the mills along the Carson River, and the mines in the Austin and Belmont areas," he said. "Add in the eastern ranches, and these in the Carson Valley, and I have to include ours in the Golden Valley,"–Chance chuckled–"and there is such a huge need of water, that this conspiracy to write the laws their way or die, may be more than our AG will really want to attack. I hope I'm wrong."

They spent a little time eating simple cold meat sandwiches, drank more than two pots of coffee, and dissected the situation into its tiniest pieces. Every piece of the pie pointed toward Burleson and O'Brien, and Chance couldn't help wonder if there wasn't something other, something more than the selfish demand that they get all the water they want, no matter what.

"Power," Chance said, wiping some horseradish from his lips and folding the napkin for the last time. "It isn't the water. Water is important, but it's the power they feel they can exert, prove they are the strongest, and their demands will grow from that. It may be water today, and it may well be food distribution tomorrow. Well, Mr. Hawkeye Byrnes, they are about to feel the strength and power of the law."

***

Chance and Byrnes left the hotel and were walking down the street toward the attorney general's office when Ira Stone and Hank Adams came around the corner from Stone's office. "You like your card games, Hawkeye, there's a pair to draw to, right there.

"Howdy, Ira and Hank, you're looking mighty fine this cold January day. I want you to meet my deputy investigator, Hawkeye Byrnes. Byrnes, this is Nevada Federal Attorney Ira Stone, and Hank Adams, owner of the stockyards in Minden."

"So, this is the gentleman you were talking about in that note you sent," Ira Stone said, shaking hands with Byrnes. "Chance says you'd like to work in the Marshal Service, eh? He and I did for many years, and if what he says is right, I think you might just fit well."

"Chance has told me many stories about you, Mr. Stone. I'm pleased to meet you, and yes, I very much want to be a marshal." The two men gave each other a full look-see, as men do, Ira knowing the tall, broad young man could take him in an instant. Both men were smiling through their eyes, glad they had the opportunity to meet.

"I'm glad we ran into each other, Ira. Got lots going on. Let's go have a beer and talk some. Hank, you need to be part of this conversation. We'll be discussing some of your customers."

They returned to the St. Charles Hotel, slipped into the elegant saloon, and found a table back away from the bar. The St. Charles was top of the line in Carson City and everything was first class, imported crystal, fine woodwork, and deep carpet were fixtures silver-rich nabobs appreciated.

Large mugs of beer were brought to the table and Chance started to lay out the conspiracy to the two men. He reminded them of the buying of legislators, of the attempted murder of the judge, of the continued threats to the man, of Spencer's attempted run and then attempted murder, and finally, the blowing up of the jail.

"I have three men in my sights right now, and I think I have enough evidence for Elmer Barlow to issue warrants, but I'd love to hear some comments from you two. What do you know about Burleson, O'Brien, and Carrington? Their money has been flowing like spring runoff."

Hank Adams explained that all three were successful ranchers, that Burleson and O'Brien demanded things be done their way, and their way only, and that Carrington was a little easier to get along with. "If what you say is true, Chance, I would have to believe that Carrington has gotten in way over his head. This isn't the man I've dealt with at the yards, not at all. Carrington lost his wife in a tragic buggy accident two years ago and he's been a different man since then.

"I think you're dead on with Burleson and O'Brien. They are big, swaggering, proud men who look down on everything and everyone. I would say one or both want to be governor and then U.S. senator." Hank Adams chuckled a bit, but his eyes weren't smiling as he said that.

"In my opinion, they're just cowards," Chance said.

Stone indicated that Spencer was used by Burleson and O'Brien to make the arrangements for payoffs and distribution of funds, keeping their names out of the picture, and the feds were already looking into the situation. "I see a conspiracy, the same as you, Chance."

"Why would the feds be interested in what appears to be a Nevada conspiracy dealing with legislative and judicial crimes?" Chance wanted to get as much as possible lined up against the men before he moved himself.

"The waters in question, at least around here, are bi-state. The Truckee River, Carson River, and most branches of the Walker River begin in California and flow to Nevada. In the east, the Humboldt River and Reese River are purely Nevada rivers, even though they are part of your conspiracy.

"It will be a long time before these water issues are settled, Chance, and what's happening in Nevada right now will be a part of the final solution. The federal government is going to be involved because of interstate water. What Amos Stanfield is trying to do will be part of the final solution, and what Burleson and company are trying to do will continue to complicate the matter for a long time.

"You being a part of Barlow's force is a blessing, my friend," Stone said. "I'm sure Elmer Barlow never heard of the problem until you laid it on his desk. Until he hired you, there wasn't one investigator on his payroll. Continue with what you're doing, from the state angle, and I'll continue what I'm doing. If you can get Barlow to issue some warrants, it will be a big help."

They spent another two mugs of beer discussing just how encompassing the problem was, just how many people may be involved, and broke up late in the afternoon. "Looks like we better make our visit with Barlow early tomorrow morning, Hawkeye. Don't want to blow beer all over the man's office." He snickered. "I'm going to go look at a couple of houses for rent. Jenny and the children will be arriving in two days and I don't have anything lined up yet."

"I ran into a deputy last night. Olsen was his name, and somehow he's connected at the hip with the sheriff. I'm gonna try to find out more about that man and maybe turn up some information on our fine Ormsby County sheriff. Micah Doyle should be breaking his butt wanting to work with us on this case, Chance. I'm gonna find out why he isn't."

***

On his way to check out a house near to town, Chance dropped in on Supreme Court Justice Amos Stanfield. "I may actually have some good news for you, Amos," he said, shaking the man's hand and slipping into one of the large wingback chairs in front of the judge's desk. "We're pretty sure the attempts on your life were engineered by Nate Burleson with some help from Seamus O'Brien, and might have them in custody in the next few days.

"How are you holding up?"

"I'm fine, Jacob, and so glad you're on this job. Even Augie Roark has calmed down some." He laughed.

"Well, we may want him to get back un-calmed, Amos. That jail explosion this morning was done by someone who has a great knowledge of explosives, and we don't know if it was one of the ranchers or if they hired someone. Byrnes wants you to move out of your home, but I'm asking, instead, that you inform Roark, and he'll keep a close eye on things. At least for the time being."

"I ain't moving out of my home," Stanfield said immediately, to Chance's chortle. "No sir. But I will tell Roark what you just said. This is almost getting out of hand, Jacob." He settled back in his large leather chair and looked deep into Jacob Chance's eyes. "I'm sorry to have gotten you into this mess, Jacob. I've taken you away from your family again, away from your ranch."

Chance couldn't help remembering how Amos Stanfield's first reaction to almost anything was its effect on others, never on himself. *Right now,* he's thinking, *this wonderful old man is more worried about me and my family, while there are forces working to have him killed. Men have tried to ambush the judge, and now, there is the possibility of a bomber working to take him out. They don't make men like Amos Stanfield very often.*

"Don't even think about that, Amos. You're a dear friend, and there is an upside to all this. Jenny and the children should be here in a day or two, and will spend several weeks. Jerrod Stockton wants me to testify on several bills he will be working through this legislative session, and my family will be right here with me.

"In fact, sir, I'm supposed to go look at a house for us, right now. I just wanted to make sure everything was right with you."

"More than right, Chance, more than right. What kind of house?"

"It's a Victorian a couple of blocks north and west of here. It will be adequate, but a bit expensive. I guess the rent fluctuates based on when the legislature is in session." He chuckled.

"That nice house directly next to mine is also mine, Jacob, and it is vacant, and the rent is free." Supreme Court Justice Amos Stanfield opened the top drawer on his massive oak desk and pulled a ring full of keys out. Taking one from the ring, he handed it across the desk. "Here, Jacob, is the key to your new home. Go make it ready for Jenny and the children. I will be so glad to see them again, and hear all the noise from a happy family next door."

"I have to pay something, Amos. We might be there for more than a month."

"You have already made that payment, Marshal Chance, many times over."

Chapter Thirteen

It was pure turmoil at the Chance ranch for two solid days and nights as Jenny and the crew tried to make the family ready for the long journey north. "I thought this would be reasonably easy to put together," Jenny said, laughing watching Buck Colby trying to get one more large package on the wagon. "All the stuff we're going to need for the trip itself will ride on top?"

"We'll be spending two nights on the trail, Jenny, so I'll have the trail stuff packed so we can get at it. Cookie will drive this wagon, you'll drive the buggy with Little Jake alongside, Mrs. Stockton will be in the back seat with Missy. The senator, Slim Crockett and I will be riding our saddle horses, so camp will be large each night."

Despite the fact it was still mid-winter, the weather was cooperating, with short sunshine-filled days and long cold but clear nights. Winds had been moderate, but those that had spent many winters in Nevada knew all that could change within minutes. "I sure hope this weather holds for another several days," Jenny said, looking at how high Colby had things piled. "A good solid norther would tip that wagon over in a heartbeat, Buck."

They were both still chuckling when Colby climbed down and finished tying off the ropes. "It's more of a circus, I think. I guess we can feel very lucky, though, about the weather. It'll be cold as all get out but at least we won't be riding through a blizzard."

Colby, Stockton, and Crockett were far more worried about who they might meet on the trail. "We cannot forget what happened to Judge Stanfield when he came down here for Christmas." Jerrod Stockton was still in a fit over Jenny and the children making the trip to

Carson City. "I'm still dead set against you going, Jennifer Chance," he said, puffing up his almost three hundred pounds and towering over her.

"I know you are, Jerrod, but I'm sure if Chance had heard about any problems, he would have sent word down to us. We haven't heard of any threats, and Chance is right there. Besides, I want to go and I want the children to know about the capital, I'm even planning on an excursion to the Comstock to see those fabulous mines."

Even though Roger Bullis ran his stables, Senator Jerrod Stockton still did all the blacksmith and forge work and was just as strong as some of the oxen he had to take care of. "Those fellers met that stagecoach with plans to kill every single person on board. You, my lovely little lady, could very well be a target, and your children as well. These people are dealing with loaded decks, Jennifer, and they know how to deal from the bottom of each one."

"Your concerns are noted, Jerrod, and that is why we are so grateful for all of you men riding with us."

"Don't play that game, Jenny. This is serious."

"I know it is, Jerrod," she said, lowering her eyes, knowing she should not have said that, particularly to this man. "The children and I will never be safer because of you and Buck and Slim. I know Cotton Phelps wanted to make the ride but with everyone down with the flu, he can't leave. I'm glad he sent us Slim Crockett." It was Crockett and Hank Adams who saved Stanfield from the killers at Christmas, and the tall, thin cowboy was now working for the Phelps ranch.

Stockton laughed. "Slim Crockett will be riding with us, but his heart and soul will be in Preston taking care of Clemmie Bullis. It's a good thing it's still winter, because I'm sure Cotton Phelps would have something to say about how much time that boy spends in town."

Buck Colby had the teams hitched, people were piling into wagons and buggies while others mounted their horses. Amid shouts of "let's go," and the crack of reins slapping the drivers, the caravan moved off. Little Jake had the reins with his proud Mama sitting alongside, and two-year-old Missy was laughing and whooping it up with the rest of the group. "After all," Jenny whispered, "this is our holiday."

Stockton rode point with Crockett riding drag, and Colby stayed between the wagon driven by Cookie leading, and the buggy. They climbed out of the Golden Valley on a clear and cold January morning, looking forward to an exciting month touring Carson City, Virginia City, and maybe getting their first ride on a railroad train.

Little Jake was seven, and between Juan Ortega, the Mexican horse breeder, and Buck Colby, the ranch foreman, he could ride like a Vaquero, rant like an American cowboy, and perform just about any job on the ranch. He had no inclination to allow his mother to drive the buggy team, and even gave her a little pat on the knee, saying, "It'll be fine, Mom."

Stockton waved Colby up to the lead and said something to him, turned his horse and rode off toward the Good Hope River. It was one of those glorious mid-winter mornings with no wind and a warm sun beating down on him. He rode to a point where the river takes a little bend and there's just the slightest willow covered peninsula protruding into the rushing water. He stepped off his horse and tied it to some of the willows, back a bit from the river.

Sure wish old Cotton Phelps was along with us on this trek. I guess we'll be okay or Chance surely would have sent word not to come. Jenny's probably right. He put his worries aside and decided to concentrate on what he did best, shoot ducks and geese.

He pulled his double-barreled shotgun from its scabbard, ducked into the willows, and just like he figured, two big mallard drakes hightailed it from the reeds. Ducks and geese were Stockton's favorite game birds to hunt and to eat, and he shot the first one, then the other, and watched where they crashed. *It's always nice to get a double.*

A couple of hours later he rode up on the caravan and handed the pair of mallards up to Cookie. "Think roast duck might taste pretty good tonight, Cookie. What do you think?"

"Sounds fine to me, senator, just fine. Maybe tomorrow you can find us a nice young antelope buck, eh?" He laughed. "All kidding aside, though, I brought enough meat for three days. We'll be fine, Jerrod."

They made camp as the sun began its dip behind the mighty Sierra Nevada, alongside a stream and with plenty of good grass for the animals. It was short work getting the tents up, a fire pit dug, and the aroma of roasting duck soon filled the air. Cookie had potatoes and fresh corn roasting over the coals as well, and there was a huge pot of coffee boiling too.

"This is what I love so much," Jenny said, as Jake settled in next to her, "on the spring drive, when we take the herd up high into those mountains, sitting near an open fire in the evening, watching the stars come out, and eating half a ton of good food." She laughed. "Your papa spent most of his life living outdoors like this, and can cook a King's Spread over open coals."

"Can I make the spring and fall drives this year, Mama? I'm a good vaquero, according to Juan. He said I'd make a good charro, someday."

"You ride and rope well, you're big and strong, I think you should ride with us from now on, Jake, and I'm sure Chance will agree. You've made the rides before but not as one of the hands. You'll be a working hand this year."

Jenny figured they heard the loud yippee clear back in Preston, and she had to spend a little time getting Missy back to sleep.

***

"If you can get me just a little bit more, Chance, I'll issue those warrants. You have made a very good case," Elmer Barlow, Nevada attorney general said, "but I'd like something with some grit on it. That information from Ted Whistler along with the statements from Monty Smith are damning, and if you can get me something with a personal tie, you'll have your warrants."

Chance and Byrnes were in the AG's office when Barlow arrived, and laid out the case, item by item. Barlow was probably right, Chance thought. Everything was from another person. Spencer was dead and he would have been a direct tie. He got the money from the ranchers and paid for the criminal acts. "I'm pretty sure we'd get a conviction on what we have, but I agree that we can make this case stronger.

"Hawkeye and I are heading out to talk with Carrington when we're through here, and based on what he says, we'll visit with Burleson and O'Brien in the next two days. I feel sure the threat on Stanfield's life is probably over, now. There aren't any more fools willing to take the job." Chance laughed.

"Amos tells me your family is coming up, Chance. Will that interfere with your work?"

"Not in the least, Barlow. Senator Stockton and my ranch foreman are riding up with them, and we'll all be here through the next session of the legislature. Stockton is bringing me some information on how Burleson and O'Brien made their approaches to the various elected officials on this water question. He has documentation, and that might just be one of the ties you're looking for."

"Wonderful," Barlow said. "You'll be fine talking with Carrington, but watch your back when you're with Burleson and O'Brien. Seamus O'Brien is a foul-mouthed back stabber, Jacob, so you two watch out."

The ride to Carrington's ranch was more than pleasant. Leaving Eagle Valley, where Carson City was located, and following along the road through Jack's Valley and into Carson Valley, they were at the base of the front range of the Sierra Nevada. One of the things that stood out was a lack of trees.

"I've ridden through sections of these mountains many times, Hawkeye," Chance said, "and every time this sight surprises me. The first time I saw the bare hills was years ago coming from San Francisco and looking down into the Lake Tahoe basin. The entire mountainsides are denuded.

"Just look at this," he said, waving his arms to encompass the hillsides. "Every tree that stood here for hundreds of years, is now holding up a mine in Virginia City. Hundreds of thousands of cords of wood now underground. Amazing."

The road led through Genoa, as the town was called. When it formed, the first real community in Nevada, and back then it was Utah Territory, it was called Mormon Station. Many of the ranches in the Carson Valley, their water fed by the Carson River, were originally laid out by the Mormons, but when Brigham Young called the saints home to Salt Lake City, the ranches were turned over to others. With many of the properties, the questions of ownership were still up in the air.

At Genoa, they crossed the river and rode through the broad plain of the valley. The Carrington ranch was before Minden, where Hank Adams had his stockyards. Huge pastures, brown with winter's ice and cold, were spread out in all directions from a large main ranch house. Spacious and tall, dressed smartly in Victorian architecture and style, the house stood out on the broad plain.

Chance and Byrnes rode up to the front as Carrington stepped onto a broad porch from the house.

"Good morning," Chance said. "Are you Henry Carrington?"

"Who's asking?" the rancher snarled, finding unexpected guests. He saw that neither man was a working cowboy, so they weren't looking for jobs, and both were well armed. His own revolver was hanging on a hook inside the door, and his rifle stood in a stand near the fireplace.

"I'm Inspector Jacob Chance, with the Nevada attorney general's office. This is my deputy, Inspector Byrnes. We'd like to talk with you for a few minutes, sir."

"Pretty busy, Chance. Maybe another time."

"Right now would be the best time, Carrington," Chance said. There was no smile, but there was that slight threat in his words. "Our conversation would have to do with murder, threats of murder, and large explosions. I'm sure you want to make time for this little talk."

Neither man had stepped from his horse, yet, as was the custom. Carrington stood on the porch looking at the two, understanding that his world may be starting to collapse, that this may be the opening salvo of a long spiral down a long slope. "All right, step down and come in. There's coffee," he said, opening the door and walking into his warm front room.

There didn't seem to be anyone else in the house, and it wasn't as clean as most ranch homes would be. Carrington's coats and hats were draped about in the living room, there were what might have been last night's supper plates still out, and Carrington himself looked as if he had slept in the clothes he was wearing.

The fire was blazing and Carrington nodded to a couple of well-upholstered chairs near the fire. Chance shook out of his bearskin coat, Byrnes slipped out of his heavy buffalo coat, and they took their seats. Carrington sat in a third chair and nodded to a Chinese man to bring coffee.

"You're late again, Sing-Mai. Bring us coffee," Carrington said, "and a bottle of whiskey." He settled into his chair, a frown etched deep into his face, but Chance was sure he could detect considerable fear in that face as well.

"What's this about murder and threats, Chance?"

Chance saw the man's hands shaking just a bit when he took a sip of coffee and decided to lay his cards on the table, and frighten the man into divulging the entire plot, if he could. "I'm investigating what appears to be a conspiracy among elements of the ranching and mining communities to buy influence in the upcoming legislative session, to assassinate Supreme Court Justice Amos Stanfield, and to cause an explosion at the Carson City jail that killed several people.

"My investigation, so far, has led me to believe that you, sir, are a part of that conspiracy, that you and others have provided money to an individual who has used that money to bribe certain members of the legislature, who has used that money to pay for an attempt on the life of Stanfield, which by the way led to four deaths, and to create an atmosphere of fear.

"Money has also been used to attempt the murder of another man, who died in the explosion I mentioned earlier." Chance sat back and took a long drink of some very good coffee. He nodded to the Chinese man for a little more and smiled at Carrington. "Care to explain any of this?"

"I'm not involved in anything of the sort. How dare you come to my house with these kinds of allegations. You can leave right now, sir. Right now," and Carrington stood up and made a move for the rifle standing close by.

Chance laid his hand on his big revolver, didn't pull the iron, and said, "Don't make this worse than it already is, Carrington. Sit down and talk to me. You're not alone in this, there are others, and I can make life a little easier for you if you tell me all about this conspiracy. Now, sit down." He nodded his head at Byrnes who got up and walked over to the fireplace and brought the rifle back to his chair.

Carrington flopped back in his large chair and watched Chance's hand move away from his weapon. Perspiration was dripping from the man's forehead, his eyes were looking all about the living room, on stuffed animal heads mounted on the walls, on beautiful Tiffany lamps that would put fine light on the natural wood-paneled walls, on carpet brought in from San Francisco that reportedly was woven in Persia.

All of this will be gone in just a few minutes, he thought, *and all because I felt as selfish about water as that fool Burleson.* Other thoughts were flashing through his mind as well. He knew if he told about Burleson and O'Brien that they would kill him in an instant, and if he didn't, everything he had ever owned would be gone. *If I tell him the story, they will kill me, and if I don't, I may as well be dead. I lose, either way.*

"What do you want, Chance?" he murmured. Chance was looking at a broken man and knew that he was about to get exactly what Barlow had asked for.

"I want you to get some paper, a pen, and ink, and write down everything you know about how money flowed to the various members of the legislature, how money flowed to Harold Spencer and for what purpose that money was to be used, and I want the names of those that provided that money, including yours."

Carrington glared at Chance, then at Byrnes, and seemed to shake from head to toe. "If I do that, I'm a dead man, Chance. They'll kill me, Chance," he almost blubbered.

"If they don't, the state may, Carrington. We're talking murder, here. I can probably keep you from the gallows, and I can provide you with protection until after the trials, but if you don't give me a full written confession with everyone's names, I can guarantee a drop through the trap door." Everyone in the room saw that visual.

One can't get more direct than that, Byrnes thought, watching both Chance and Carrington. Byrnes had been in law enforcement long enough to know that he had just watched a master at work. *This guy is about to write himself a long-term stay in prison and Chance didn't have to say any more than a hundred words. I better remember this day for a long time if I'm going to join the Marshal Service.*

***

Carrington called his ranch foreman in and told him to keep an eye on the place, that he'd be back as soon as he could, and mounted up for the ride back to Carson City. Jacob Chance rode alongside him and Hawkeye Byrnes rode about two hundred yards or so behind them. Chance had a three-page confession tucked inside his bearskin coat and could not feel the winter's cold because of his own warm thoughts.

***

Barlow read the confession, signed by Carrington and witnessed by both Chance and Byrnes, and smiled broadly. He called his secretary in and asked him to take a note to the U.S. attorney, Ira Stone, inviting Stone for a most important meeting. "I want you and Byrnes here with me when Stone reads this," he said to Chance, waving the three pages in front of him. "What did you do, Chance, stick a revolver in his ear and pull the hammer back?"

"Never touched the man, never threatened the man," Chance drawled out, hoping that Barlow was trying for a little joke. "I don't work that way when it isn't necessary." He scowled. "Byrnes'll back me up on that, and so will that Chinaman pouring our coffee. I told the man we had enough evidence to convict, that it was an open murder charge, and that he would hang for sure unless he cooperated."

"That's the truth," Byrnes said, quickly. "I've never seen anything like it, General Barlow, in all my years carrying a badge. Chance looked the man in the eye and simply spelled it out, one charge at a time." He laughed, and said, "I expected to see a little yellow puddle at any time dripping from that chair."

Barlow roared at that, Chance reddened some, and Byrnes chuckled. Barlow opened an ornate wooden box on his desk and offered cigars around. "Get these straight from Virginia, gentlemen, please indulge."

The room was filled with a fragrant blue cloud when Ira Stone arrived. Before anything was said, Barlow offered the U.S. attorney a cigar and a broad smile. "These boys just made my day, Ira, and I'm about to make yours."

Ira Stone clamped the cigar in his teeth and had it about half chewed away before he finished reading the confession from Carrington. Chance was chuckling, trying to remember if he had ever seen Stone actually light one of his cigars. "We need to keep this man alive, Barlow. A written confession is excellent, and any judge will back me up on that, but if you can put Carrington on the stand and have him actually say these things," he paused for half a second, "well, you'll put about five notches on your resume.

"If you would be kind enough to make your entire file available to me, I plan to add several serious federal charges to what you will do." Stone got a nod from Barlow, and kept right on talking. "When are Jenny and the kids coming, Jacob? I need to have a long talk with that woman. You tell people you're retired, Chance, and then you take all these dangerous little jobs.

"I'm going to give that woman some special powers, that only a U.S. attorney can give, by the way, and she will have the authority to keep you on your ranch, with severe penalties if you don't." There was general laughter in the room as the meeting broke up.

"This is one of the things you might want to think about, Hawkeye," Chance said later that day. "Being a lawman with a large jurisdiction, such as a U.S. marshal would have, is not conducive to having a wife and children. Thinking of a wife and children at a critical point could get you killed, could endanger innocents."

"I've made that decision, Chance," he said. "I know I'm going to want a wife, maybe even children, but that will be down the line some. When I get older, like you did," he said, ducking a big fisted up paw aimed at his jaw.

Chapter Fourteen

"Just one more day, children, and we'll be with your father." Camp was in an open area, but near water. The men went out to find wood for the fires, and Jenny and Eileen Stockton were preparing the camp. "This has been a wonderful adventure," she said. "I'm so glad you and Jerrod finally tied the knot."

She laughed. "He teases that I took advantage of him, and I'll never tell him otherwise. I fell for that monster of a man the minute I saw him. He can be the most tender, most caring man I've ever known, and turn right around and hammer a piece of steel into something useful, or pick up something that weighs more than he does.

"He built that house we're living in, almost by himself, Jenny, and dug the well too. He doesn't know it yet, and I don't want to tell him until we get to Carson City, but I'm pretty sure we're going to have a little Jerrod running around soon."

"Ah! That's wonderful," Jenny cried. "I won't say a word. He'll be a puddle of unset jelly when you tell him." She laughed. "This is wonderful."

Cookie put together a banquet that night and many a song was sung around the campfire before the exhausted bunch finally tucked themselves in. There wasn't any antelope, but Cookie had brought half of a beef tenderloin and cut it into thick steaks and cooked them over open coals.

He topped that off with fresh apple pies after Jerrod had taken another little ride out from the caravan and found some wild apple trees alongside a stream. "They aren't the biggest apples in the world, Cookie, but I think I got enough for a pie or two." He did, and the pies were gone in a flash.

Morning was bright, bitter cold again, but with no wind and no impending storm. "I want to ride with Cookie today," Little Jake said, as the teams were put together and the loads tied off. "I like it when he tells stories."

"That's fine, honey," Jenny said. "Elaine, why don't you and Missy ride up front with me and we can chatter away all day." She looked over to Jerrod Stockton and asked about how far out they were from Carson City.

"We'll be coming into town about midday, Jenny. We need to be very cautious today. If those bastards," and he stopped immediately, almost gasped, "sorry, oh, my, I didn't mean to say that."

"It's okay, Jerrod, I've heard it before," Jenny said.

"Oh, my," he said again. "If those men who tried to kill the judge know you're coming to town, they just might try something. This is why I've said you shouldn't be here. It's too dangerous."

"With you and Slim and Buck, I feel pretty safe, Jerrod. Besides, I want to sit in the Senate gallery and hear you give a speech. Just watch your language." She laughed, and Stockton turned as red as a man could, snarling something about getting these blasted wagons moving, the sun will be going down soon, and the horses seem lame, and he finally just mounted his horse and rode off, leaving the women laughing hard.

"You were kind of tough on him, Jenny, but he'll get over it." Elaine laughed, climbing into the buggy. Jenny handed up Missy and joined her, taking up the reins and clucking the horses into motion. "We'll be riding right along the Carson River today, Elaine. I've been in this part of the country. We bring the cattle through here then loop south into Minden and Hank Adams' stockyards. It's a beautiful ride."

***

Chance rode down from the new house with Amos Stanfield in the morning. "How do you like your new home, Jacob?" the judge asked, settling into the cart's upholstered seat. Chance rode alongside the high wheeled cart.

"We're gonna be mighty comfortable, Amos, thank you. Did you get a letter from Elmer Barlow?"

"I did, indeed, yes I did. That was some fine work, Chance, and I have to tell you I feel much better today, knowing that you've ended this problem."

"Don't get ahead of yourself, Amos," Chance said, getting very serious. "It isn't ended, believe me. Seamus O'Brien is one dangerous man and Nate Burleson is equally to be feared. No, sir, this isn't over. Hawkeye told me that O'Brien is an old miner and powder monkey, and he might have been the one who blew up the jail. He is not in custody, Amos.

"And, according to Carrington, it was Nate Burleson who set up the hit on you on your ride to Preston, and he isn't in custody either. Hawkeye and I have a lot of work left to do before you're truly a safe man. I understand you are about to make public the supreme court opinion on Nevada water policy."

"I am, Jacob. It's written and I will publish it later today, well before the legislature meets, and it will be the law of the land at that point. After that, there would be no valid reason for anyone to want me dead, sir."

Chance laughed at that comment, thinking about the many men sitting behind bars in various jails and prisons about the west that would gladly shoot the judge. "Jenny and the kids should be coming into town later today, Amos. Would you be kind enough to have supper with us? This will a much happier time than when you were in Preston over Christmas."

"I'd like that, Jacob. Let me know what time," he said, getting his team turned into the stables near the supreme court building. Chance rode on north on Carson Street, planning to have breakfast at the Mexican cantina with Hawkeye.

***

Hawkeye Byrnes was up early and reverted to his old self of being a sheriff, and saddled his horse for a ride around town at sunrise. Unlike a ranch that gets started well before sunrise, or a mining community that seems to be working around the clock, Carson City was a late rising village. Byrnes had the streets to himself as he rode up one street and back down another, enjoying the bitter cold without a wind, and smelling the smoke from first fires.

He had made the turn onto Telegraph Street, working his way north to Carson Street, when he was hailed by a rider coming up from behind. He turned his horse and watched as Deputy Olsen came riding up. "What are you doing, Byrnes?"

"Well, my beer-drinking Deputy Olsen, good morning to you, too," Hawkeye said. "Guess it is that I can ride around town about anytime I want." Olsen tightened up at the comment, had a grim look on his face, and rode right up to Byrnes, stopping his horse just before physically touching.

"Guess you can," he snarled. "Sheriff wants you and Chance to move your prisoners out of our temporary jail. Wants 'em gone by noon today."

"I'm sure if he makes that request known to the attorney general, something will happen." Byrnes snickered. *You're a deputy sheriff, not the sheriff, and I'm a deputy attorney general investigator, not the attorney general, so I'd suggest leaving things like that to those in charge.*

"You on your way to the Silver Star for a cold beer? I'm heading that way for some coffee."

"Go to hell, Byrnes," Olsen snarled, jerking his horse around and riding back east along Telegraph Street.

Byrnes was still snickering when he walked into the saloon. "How about some of your good coffee, Ned Trimble. It's a little chilly out there this morning." He slipped out of his buffalo robe coat and warmed his hands at the large pot belly stove in the center of the room. "Sure glad there's no wind today."

"Hope that last storm be the last one for a while," Trimble said, bringing a mug of coffee. "I hear you and that marshal arrested old Henry Carrington. He the one trying to kill old Judge Stanfield?"

"We have Carrington in custody, Trimble, but he hasn't been found guilty of anything, yet. Hopefully, he'll have some company soon. What do you know about this Deputy Olsen? He worked with Sheriff Doyle long?"

"Naw, maybe six months or so. Not very bright, and likes his beer. Thinks he's something special with that badge and all. He isn't worth thinking about, Hawkeye. Doyle now, that's another question."

"Okay, Ned, I just asked the question." Byrnes snickered, watching Trimble's eyes brighten with the humor of the conversation. *He's gonna have some fun with me and make me work to get what he really wants me to know. This old guy would be fun to play poker with.*

"I can't give you honest to God proof, Hawkeye, but it's been talked about for some time around town that Doyle works for Seamus O'Brien and Nate Burleson more than he works for Orsmby County, that he's been on their payroll for years."

"That would answer some of my questions, Ned. I wouldn't spread that around too much, if I were you. People that associate with O'Brien and Burleson keep turning up dead, but I do thank you."

Byrnes finished his coffee, fought his way into that big buffalo robe coat and headed up to the cantina for breakfast with Marshal Chance. *Olsen's just a blow-hard, I guess, so I won't waste any more time on him, but Doyle's taking money from the ranchers, and that worries me. He wants Carrington and some of our other people out of his hair, and I think we better get them out. They just might not be very safe there.*

***

"I thought I had a good handle on eating Mexican food, but you might as well be Mexican the way you eat, Hawkeye," Chance said as they were enjoying a couple of platters full of huevos rancheros.

"You forget I was born in El Paso and raised in New Mexico, mi compadre." Byrnes snickered. "When you start eating this stuff as a baby, it ain't hot, it's good. What do you think about what old Ned Trimble told me about Sheriff Doyle?"

"I think we need to get our people out of there as soon as possible, one, and we need to find out a little bit more about that. Carrington didn't mention that in his long report for us."

"What time's your family coming in?"

"Late this afternoon, I think. Haven't heard anything, so they must be doing okay. With Jerrod Stockton and my ranch foreman riding with them, and that cowboy, Slim Crockett along, I know they're safe. You'll like Crockett, he's a deep-down southerner like you. Talks funny, like you, too," he said, getting a scowl back from Hawkeye, and laughing back at him.

Chapter Fifteen

Seamus O'Brien watched the dust from a rider coming toward his ranch at a full gallop and wondered who would ride that hard and why. The rider turned off the main road onto the lane that led to the O'Brien ranch house and the big man recognized the Carrington ranch foreman as he reined his horse to a sliding stop, flying out of the saddle.

"There's big trouble, O'Brien," he yelled as his boots hit the dust. "Mr. Carrington has been arrested by that marshal and taken to Carson City. He told me last week that if this ever happened I should tell you right away. What should we do?"

"You did right, Oscar. Go back to the ranch and keep it running like any other day. I'll take care of things. You'll hear from me soon. And walk that horse back, don't kill it." O'Brien was known as one of the meanest men in the area, but not to his animals. More than one ranch hand had been ordered off the property for abuse of an animal. Oscar nodded, remounted, and rode off back to Carrington's as O'Brien stepped into his house quickly.

"So," he muttered, throwing a log on the fire, "they went for the weak one first. Typical, I guess. Will Burleson or I be next?" He strapped a gun belt on, slipped into a heavy winter coat, and walked out of the house and toward the barn to mount up for the ride to Carson City. "They'll expect me to go to Burleson's, but I'm going to take this fight to them, see how they like that."

He knew that every plan the group made had failed, every chance they took to either kill Stanfield or stop the process had failed, but he simply would not accept that failure. It was not in his nature to roll over despite overwhelming evidence that what they were attempting simply wasn't going to happen. He had lived with the identity of 'hard-headed Irisher' all his life, and seemed to be willing to prove the point in this fight.

He left his horse at a stables and walked to the Silver Spur. He motioned to Dirty Dick Robinette to join him at a table near the front window, and to the barman to bring him a bottle and a couple of glasses. "I need a man that don't like to talk and a hiding place that's just as quiet, Robinette."

Dirty Dick wanted to say something about the fact they had just about used up the inventory of men, but didn't. "Old Squeaky Simon's on the loose, Seamus, and I've got that cabin out toward the canyon. Were you behind that explosion the other morning?"

"What explosion?" O'Brien snarled, meaning, you better keep your mouth shut. "Cabin locked?"

"No. Silas was staying there before he disappeared. Ride out past Empire and follow the railroad into the canyon, and you'll see it back off a ways."

"Tell anyone about this and I'll be eating your liver for supper. Get Squeaky for me," O'Brien said, and poured himself another whiskey. *I hope I don't regret coming to Robinette like this. Man can't keep his mouth shut and I can't go to Burleson. There's only one way out of this and I can't let anyone else know what I'm going to do.*

***

When the caravan reached the railroad tracks, at a point called Moundhouse, the tracks headed north into the Virginia Range and up the long grade to Virginia City. Jerrod Stockton turned the group southwest and followed the tracks through the Carson River canyon.

The road was well used and they were mixed in with others, some heading to the Comstock, some following the road to the capital. The river was running strong and they passed several large ore mills on their trek.

The mines in Virginia City, some well over two thousand feet deep, were belching out hundreds of thousands of tons of raw ore daily, and train load after train load deposited that rock at these mills.

"I've never seen anything like this in my life," Jenny said. "The immensity is overpowering, the noise is incredible, and I'm overwhelmed." She chuckled at the way all of that came out. "All of this for a piece of gold," she said, quietly.

"No, Jenny, not a piece of gold, but a mountain of silver and gold." Jerrod Stockton had spent hours on the Comstock, had been on tours of some of the mines, knew John Mackay and James Fair, the Comstock Silver Barons, personally, and like so many, was more than impressed with what those mines produced.

"When we get into town, we'll drive right past a large building built of local stone, that houses the U.S. Mint, and great ingots, literally bars of silver and gold, are brought to the mint where thousands of dollars' worth of coins are stamped daily. No, Jenny, not just a piece of gold, an entire mountain of silver and gold."

Stockton sent Buck Colby ahead to find Chance and let him know how close they were. "I think we're safe for these last five miles or so," he said. "Slim, you ride a few yards behind the buggy and I'll ride a few yards in front of the wagon, and everyone keep a sharp lookout."

They rode past some very active mills turning out hundreds of pounds of silver and gold daily, and were amazed by the number of people they passed on the road into the capital. "Just too many people for someone to try something, I think," Stockton mused, watching all the activity.

Within the hour they saw a lone rider approaching and Stockton took off his beat up old floppy hat and waved it high. "There he is, Jenny, Jacob Chance, U.S. marshal, riding for his woman," he howled, laughing and waving some more. Chance rode right past him and didn't pull up until he was alongside Jenny's buggy. Chance bailed off his big Morgan and lifted Jenny right out of the buggy, hugging and kissing her like he hadn't seen her in years.

Little Jake piled off Cookie's wagon and ran to his dad, grabbing him by a leg and hugging, and all the people traveling to Carson City one way and Virginia City the other way got quite a show. Some yelled and waved in delight, some frowned and squalled at being slowed down.

After hugging Jenny and the kids, he got the mini wagon train back underway, tying off his horse to the buggy, sending Elaine to the back seat and doing the driving himself. "Looks like you had an easy trip up," he said after things calmed down. "Amos Stanfield has a very nice house waiting for you, and Ira Stone will be hosting us at supper tonight."

"It's been tiring, Chance, I guess because we feared danger all the time, but we had a good trip. Little Jake's been driving Cookie's wagon all day, and Missy has been a chatter-box the whole time, pointing at everything. I'm so glad to see you, to be with you, and know that you're safe."

"There's somebody you're gonna meet shortly who you'll love for sure. I found him in Virginia City and claimed him for my own. His name is Hawkeye, can you beat that? And he's my deputy investigator right now. Ira's already working to get him in the Marshal Service. He's gonna be a good one."

Jenny thought Chance had been saving up for all the time he'd been gone and just wouldn't stop talking the entire rest of the way into town. It gave her an opportunity to look at this town called the capital of Nevada. She was amazed by the railroad works and sounds, and loved the look of the U.S. Mint building. She called it more than impressive, and was shocked at the amount of people out and about.

"I've never seen this many people in my life," she whispered to Chance as they made their way through the heavy traffic. Before getting into the city proper, he pulled the buggy ahead of the wagon so he could lead the way through the maze of streets and into the yards at the Stanfield properties.

"I was a very young girl when Papa brought us to Nevada and we settled in the Golden Valley. I might be able to say I'm close to being a native, and I've never seen this many people, never seen this much activity. Even when we bring the herds up, Chance, we've never come to Carson City.

"We drive the herd to Minden, do our business with Hank Adams and get right back on the trail to Preston." Her eyes were trying to see everything all at the same time, and she found herself jabbering about what she was seeing. "Just tell me to be quiet, Chance," she said with a chuckle.

They passed by a construction project that Chance pointed out. "That's where the governor will be living soon," he said. Stanfield and his law clerk Augie Roark were waiting for the entourage and had moved things about making room for the buggy and wagon and all the horses.

***

Two men rode northeast out of town shortly after the Chance troupe rode through Carson City, bound for that same canyon along the Carson River. "If I hear that you've said one word about what I'm doing, you'll find yourself one dead little man. You understand that?" Seamus O'Brien snarled, moving the horses off the main trail and up into a narrow canyon that opened into a snow covered meadow. A small cabin stood in a grove of trees at the end of the meadow with a weather barn and corral off to the side.

"You've made your point, O'Brien. I'll keep my end of the bargain, you make sure you keep yours." Squeaky Simon was nearing fifty years old, and got his name from a habit he had of making strange noises through his nose when he blew it or tried to breath hard. He was mean mannered, had few friends, and was known to carry a knife that would make Jim Bowie take a second look. "How long is this gonna take?"

"Just a few days, probably. Depends on whether or not the judge caves in right away or tries to be a tough old man. Don't let me down," O'Brien said, riding up to the front of the cabin and stepping off his horse.

"I already said I wouldn't. You gettin' second thoughts, get 'em out in the open, O'Brien. I don't like the constant questioning of me. Keep it up, you can find somebody else for this."

"Take it easy, Squeaky, I'm just making sure. Been screwed over by others, and I don't much care for that. Let's get the fire lit and get some coffee on, and I'll leave you be."

There was wood stacked by the fireplace, kindling as well, and Squeaky had a roaring fire popping in no time, with a pot of coffee hanging on one of the hooks over the fire. "Looks to be a fair cabin," Squeaky said. "That fool Spade Dooley spent some time here before he got knocked off, and Dirty Dick's cousin Silas bunked here, too."

"You got plenty of food, Squeaky, there's good whiskey in the cabinet, and I'll be back with the goods in the next day or two. You're gettin' good money for this, so don't let me down," O'Brien said one more time. He walked out, mounted up, and rode back to Carson City with a broad smile. *Your days are numbered, Amos Stanfield. You and that so-called marshal will beg me soon, beg, grovel, and give me my water. It's on my property, it's mine.*

***

Ira Stone went all-out for his welcome home banquet later that evening. While the Chance family, Judge Stanfield, and the Stocktons were enjoying a feast at the St. Charles Hotel,

Slim Crockett took the time to look over Carson City, and Cookie was resupplying the wagon for the long haul back to Preston.

Crockett had taken a room at a smaller hotel and planned to stay in the capital just a day or two before heading back to Preston and his job with Cotton Phelps. Or, maybe to get back to Clementine Bullis. *There are places in Texas that get mighty cold, but this Nevada cold is more than I want. Maybe I'll just marry up with that pretty little girl and we'll head back to southeast Texas.* He rode through the capital with a wide smile.

On the way north he'd got an earful from Senator Stockton on exactly what the problems were that ranchers and others would be facing if Judge Stanfield wasn't able to write and present his majority opinion to the court. Chance had taken him aside when they arrived in town and asked that he keep his ears open for any discussion about either the water law or the judge, and Hawkeye Byrnes had given him a couple of good ideas on where to get a good meal and a fair treatment at the saloons.

Being the good son of Texas, Crockett was sitting at a small table in one of the many Mexican restaurants in the city when he heard a man discussing the arrest of Henry Carrington. "That marshal and his deputy just rode onto the ranch, fancy as all get out, with their shiny badges and all, and put old Mr. Carrington in handcuffs and hauled him off. Just like that," the man said, kicking back a shot of tequila and pouring a second one.

"Why would they arrest old Henry?" one of the cowboys said. "I never rode for the man, but I've heard good things about him. You ride for him, Oscar, why'd they do that?"

"Said he was one of them what blew up the jail the other night and killed those prisoners. I heard that Virginia City sheriff say that." Conversation turned to other topics and Crockett tucked the information away and had a fine supper. He drifted down to the Silver Star after, and slipped up to the bar.

"I think I want a cold beer to take out some of them chilies," he said to the barman, "and a good cigar. "Whewee, that lady knows how to make Texas chili." He laughed.

"Musta ate at Rosie's Cantina, eh, cowboy? I better get you two beers for a starter." He joined in the laughter, opening a box of cigars for Crockett. "You sound like you're from way down there in Texas somewhere."

"Yeah, come up here from El Paso looking for a good ranch to settle onto." He didn't intend to tell anyone he already had a job, hoping maybe somebody would talk about the ranchers involved in the conspiracy. "Anybody hirin'?" he asked.

"Looks like the whole crew will be leaving Carrington's ranch," the barman said. "You might have better luck checking in at the Adams' Stockyards. They'd know first about openings, I think."

"Obliged," Crockett said, motioning for another glass of beer. He saw the barman say something to the gambler running one of the card tables, and the man got up and walked right up to him.

"Hear you might be looking for some work, cowboy," he said, getting a vigorous nod back. "My name's Dick Robinette and I know a man what's lookin' for someone can handle a gun. You be interested in something like that?"

"I'm listening," Crockett said, taking a long pull on his beer. He thought this Robinette character was about as crooked as any he'd seen. *Won't put a dime's trust in this yahoo,* he thought. "Man need protection from somebody?"

"That's about the size of it. I'm plannin' on meeting him early in the morning, if you'd like to be around. Seamus O'Brien runs a fair spread, but he's looking to guard or protect something. He's coming in about five tomorrow morning, he said, if you want to check with him."

"Thanks, Robinette, I'll be here," Crockett said. "Might just play a hand or two with you before I call it a night," he said, walking toward Robinette's table, lighting a new cigar, and putting a few gold coins on the table.

Five hands later, Crockett stood from the table tucking about a hundred dollars into his poke. "Thanks again, Robinette," he said, and sauntered out the door. *That man's a sleazy bastard but I've played with too many of them. He'll never know how I made those cards of mine just show up.* He chuckled, finding his horse for the short ride to where Byrnes was staying.

***

"You're sure that he said it was O'Brien he would be meeting? O'Brien and Burleson are the other two ranchers involved in this conspiracy to kill Stanfield. We're pretty sure it was Burleson's money that set up the attempt on the stagecoach you were on. These boys play for keeps," Byrnes said.

"Robinette said he thought O'Brien was looking to guard or protect something. Might be worth it to meet up with the man."

"O'Brien wouldn't connect you to either me or Chance, so it might very well be a way to find out what that man's a-plannin'," Byrnes said with a chuckle. "I'm meeting with Chance at breakfast, so you better plan on joinin' us, after your meeting with O'Brien." He paced around the small hotel room for a minute, Crockett figuring he was in pretty deep thought.

"Of the bunch of them ranchers, Seamus O'Brien is the one that would be the meanest and dirtiest. Burleson would pay for something to be done, while O'Brien would simply go out and do it. He's not a gunfighter, Slim, he's a saloon bruiser, a hard-knuckles, heavy booted brawler, so keep yourself ready. He gets mighty angry mighty fast, and always carries a big knife."

"I'll remember that," Crockett said, shaking Byrnes' hand and heading back to his hotel and a quick sleep before an early morning meeting.

Chapter Sixteen

"You told somebody I was gonna be here? Damn you, Robinette," and Dirty Dick Robinette went flying across the mostly empty Silver Star Saloon, crashing through tables and chairs, rolling up in a heap near the stairway. He was trying to get his legs and feet under him when a massive boot thundered into his ribs and he was flattened. A second boot hurled into his head, once, twice, and Robinette died from a caved in skull.

There was absolute silence in the saloon, Ned Trimble, the late-night barman, stood as a silent sentry behind the plank, and Slim Crockett eased himself toward the door. *Ten seconds earlier and I would have been in the middle of that.* Crockett had walked in just as O'Brien threw that massive right fist into Dirty Dick's face and sent him flying. *Nobody but Robinette knew I was coming, I don't know a soul in here, so I think I might just stay for a couple of minutes and see what develops.*

Crockett stopped just inside the door and watched as people slowly came back to life, picking up drinks, shuffling cards, lighting cigars. Slim Crockett asked Ned Trimble for a cup of coffee. "Want something in it?" Trimble asked, getting the no sign and a slight grin back.

"One of you fools supposed to meet with me this morning?" O'Brien snarled, pointing around at the few men still in the saloon. Nobody said a word and the huge rancher ordered a whiskey and stood at the bar. "This is what's gonna happen to the next man that decides to go against me," he snarled, slamming the glass down. He poured another shot, downed it at once, and stomped out the bat-wing doors into another cold, blustery mid-winter morning.

"That's one mean sumbitch," Slim said to Trimble. "Is he a regular?"

"That's Seamus O'Brien, has a big ranch south of here, in the Carson Valley. The dead one is Dirty Dick Robinette, who once was a gambler at these tables and was one of the owners of the saloon."

"Looks like he picked the wrong man to cheat," Crockett said, getting another cup of hot coffee.

"He wasn't cheatin' at cards, cowboy, he just never knew when to keep his stupid mouth shut." Trimble walked down the bar and called to a couple of the men standing around Robinette's body. "How about you boys carting that poor boy's body down to the doc's. See if you can find a deputy, too."

Slim Crockett stayed at the Silver Star for another hour or so, sipping coffee, and watching the limited action. Deputy Gerald Olsen showed up about half an hour after Robinette's body was dragged down to the doctor's office, and talked with Trimble for a couple of minutes, and ambled out.

Now, there's a real lawman. Crockett chuckled to himself. *Didn't write down a single word, didn't ask a single question, never looked another man in the eye. Betcha Marshal Chance will enjoy what I'm gonna tell him.*

***

"Mornin' marshal, mornin' Hawkeye," Crockett said, swinging his leg over a chair and dropping down into it. "Cold out there."

"It is that, Crockett," Chance said. "Make your meeting with O'Brien?"

"Well," that old Texas cowboy drawled out, "I did see the man. He killed the gambler just as I walked in the door, growled at everyone there, drank a bit, and hightailed it out the door. Murder don't seem to mean much in this old town," he said, with just the hint of a smile coming across his face. "Deputy came in, made sure the murder did actually happen, and left. I guess they don't plan to do much about it."

"I guess we don't know any more than we did," Chance said. "When are you heading back to Preston?"

"Thought I'd look around this old town today and leave out in the morning. Mr. Phelps didn't want me to be gone too long," he said.

"I bet Clemmie didn't either." Chance chuckled, seeing the cowboy stiffen up some. "I'll put together a little packet for you to carry back to Alvarado and Bullis, so plan on breakfast tomorrow before you take off."

Crockett hadn't said anything, but had plans to ride to Virginia City, to see that fabulous town where the streets were paved with silver ore. He finished his breakfast, listening to Chance and Byrnes talk about how they planned to meet with Burleson, arrest the man, and hopefully find O'Brien as well. *They better take a couple of coon dogs and half a dozen shotguns if they go after that fool.*

***

"Y ou want that job or not, Oscar. You ain't gonna be working here much longer," O'Brien barked. "Pay is five hundred, should give you enough money to get out of this part of the country. Take it or leave it."

"I'll take it, Mr. O'Brien, as long as I don't have to do no killing."

"No killing, Oscar, just taking," O'Brien said. They went into Carrington's big house and sat in the warm kitchen. The Chinese cook had coffee ready in minutes, and brought out a platter of sweet rolls and jam for the men.

"That marshal is gonna be too busy to think about that darlin' little boy of his, Oscar. The most important thing to remember is to keep that kid alive. He ain't no good to anyone if he's dead. You snatch that boy and ride hard to that cabin we talked about. Don't worry about trying to hide your trail. There's so much traffic on that road ain't nobody be able to trail you."

"I hope you're right about the marshal not being with the woman and kids. I'm not a gunman, Mr. O'Brien, but I know I can snatch a kid. I'll just throw him over the saddle and run like the wind."

"The only people know about this is you and me, Oscar, so if I hear about it from someone, I'm gonna kill you long and slow. Now, git," he snarled, motioning the Chinese cook for more coffee and some more sweet rolls. He watched Oscar mount up and ride off toward Carson City and figured he might just make himself known around Carson himself.

If people see me when that kid is snatched, they sure as hell can't blame me. He laughed, munching on a roll. *I might just hire that Chinaman.* The thought that his days as a rancher might be numbered never entered his mind.

O'Brien made a leisurely trip across the north end of the Carson Valley and over what some call Duck Hill into the Eagle Valley. His first stop in Carson City was Rosa's Cantina for something to eat.

"Hello, Micah, how are you this fine winter morning?" O'Brien said, sitting across the table from the shcriff. "I heard what happened to your jail. Must have been a hell of a mess."

"There's talk you had something to do with that, Seamus. According to Ned Trimble you killed Dirty Dick Robinette this morning, too."

"Lot of people talking too much, Doyle. You just remember what our deal is, remember who slips those gold coins into your purse from time to time, and stay the hell out of my business."

"I remember, O'Brien, but three people died in that explosion, and Dirty Dick was pretty well liked. Lots of people talking and some wondering why I haven't done anything. On top of that, you've got that damned marshal getting into everything. I can't keep him away from you, Seamus. Not at all."

"I'll take care of that marshal, Micah, you just remember to keep your damned mouth shut. Where you putting your prisoners now that you got no jail?" He laughed, but really wanted to know.

"My prisoners are being taken care of over at Jensen's stables."

"What other prisoners would there be?" O'Brien asked.

"That marshal and the Virginia City sheriff are now working for the attorney general, and they have what they call their prisoners settled in at the state prison. Good for them. Means I don't have to feed them," he said, still angry at the way Byrnes had talked to him.

"Now, listen, Micah. Just who would be their prisoners?" O'Brien wanted another shot at killing Smith and Sammy Lauck.

"They brought Sammy Lauck down from Virginia City and that feller Monty Smith who was supposedly gonna kill Spencer. They were hurt pretty bad in the explosion, and they're in the prison now." Doyle didn't even mention the fact that Henry Carrington was now settled in at the state prison.

O'Brien finished his meal, said goodbye to the sheriff, and walked down the street toward the Silver Star. There was considerable traffic on this cold day, and he wondered if that woman would take the children out. "Oscar's not very bright, but Carrington always said if you told him what to do, he would do it," he was mumbling, walking into the warm, smoky saloon.

"Whiskey," he snarled at the barman, glancing around to see who might be there. He saw a new man at the gambling table, and thought he recognized him from the

Washoe Club in Virginia City. He chuckled. "That didn't take long."

***

"Come on children, hurry. We'll take the buggy downtown and I'll show you where all the gold and silver from the Comstock is turned into bright shiny coins." Augie Roark had pleaded with Amos Stanfield and Jacob Chance to be allowed to show off the capital city to Jennifer and children. "We'll see the State Capitol building, and we'll spend some time at the railroad station."

Little Jake was as excited as a seven-year-old can get, had questions piling up on questions for Roark, while little Missy was trying to make sense of all the uproar. She was a placid child, not rambunctious like Jake, and would probably sleep through most of the tour, Jenny hoped.

Chance demanded just one stipulation, that Roark carried a sidearm, which the large man said he would. "I have Judge Stanfield's best chariot ready for you," he said, escorting the family down the long stairway to the street below. "A pair of fine dancing ponies are waiting," the young man said, with a generous smile.

The day was cold, almost gloomy, Jennifer thought, with little sunshine and too much wind. She held Missy in her lap and Jake sat up front with Augie Roark, everyone bundled in wool blankets. Sprinkles of snow began falling and the wind eased off some as the tour began. They drove slowly as they passed the Virginia and Truckee Railroad works, saw engines steaming up, and marveled at the beauty of the engines and various rail cars.

"Will we get to ride on the train, Ma?" Little Jake asked, his eyes spinning as he tried to see everything all at the same time. One of the engines gave a mighty blast of its whistle and began to chug from the station. "Wow," is all he could manage to get out. Missy clung to her mother, but watched all the happenings with as much interest as her big brother. The engine gave another whistle and she giggled and clapped, but clung tight.

"Those rails are almost laid all the way to Reno," Roark said, "and of course go all the way to the Comstock. The company is planning on driving the rails into Minden, probably starting this spring. It's quite an enterprise. You can go, by rail, all the way from Virginia City to San Francisco. Well, actually, Sacramento."

They watched the train leave the depot and Roark turned the horses and began to drive them down Carson Street, and they passed the U.S. Mint. "We can't go in the mint," Roark said, but we can stop and walk around the beautiful building, if you like."

"Let's just drive by, Mr. Roark," Jennifer said. "I'm afraid it's just too cold for us to be out too much longer. Maybe a stop near a café for something warm, and then back to the house, if you don't mind."

"There's a very nice lunch room not too far south of the Capitol. Hot chocolate for the children and hot coffee for us, eh?" He laughed, twitching the buggy whip and getting the horses moving a bit faster. The wind died down considerably but the snow started falling with a great desire. "It'll be a mess around town later, if this snow keeps up like this."

They didn't notice the lean cowboy riding not too far behind them. When Augie Roark and Little Jake jumped down from the buggy and Augie went to help Jennifer and Missy down, the cowboy spurred his horse, leaned far out of the saddle and made a grab for Little Jake, snatching him by his jacket. Augie dove for the boy, grabbing his legs, and hung on, both of them being dragged down the street.

The buttons on Little Jake's jacket popped, one, two, three, and he and Augie fell and rolled into the muddy street, barely evading the sharp horses' hooves. The cowboy kept riding and was well out of sight by the time

Augie was able to get to his feet. He grabbed Little Jake and hugged him tight, asking if he was hurt.

"No," he said, shaking with fright and cold. His jacket was gone, his shirt was ripped right down the front, and he was shivering with cold. Jennifer and Missy were standing near the side of the buggy, still screaming their fright. Roark got everyone back in the buggy and drove the team hard and fast back to their home.

Roark got the fires going good while Jennifer made a big pot of coffee and cups of chocolate for the children. She was still shaking with fright and trying to calm Missy down when she heard Chance come storming through the doors. He grabbed her and just held on, rubbing her back very gently, squeezing hard, almost sobbing his fright.

"I was in Stanfield's office when someone ran in with the news. I got here as quickly as I could. Is everyone okay? Tell me what happened." He held her tight, rocked back and forth, trying to calm her down, trying to calm himself, and letting her hug him as tightly as she wanted. It was probably a full two minutes before they separated.

She poured coffee for the adults and hot chocolate for the children and everyone sat at the big kitchen table, all trying to talk at the same time. "Okay, let's take it easy now," Chance said with a smile. "Roark, what happened?"

Roark told it as best he could remember, but simply never got a look at the cowboy. "Just a typical lean cowboy. I never saw his face. He rode up fast, leaned out of the saddle and grabbed Jake. I was really lucky to be able to grab Jake's legs and hold on. That cowboy was riding hard and never let go of Jake's jacket.

"The only thing that stood out about the man was his coat. He was wearing a blanket coat, fringes and all. I've seen them in Wyoming and Colorado country."

"That'll be good to remember, Roark. Thank you for saving our son," Chance said, shaking his hand. "Hawkeye is trying to find some witnesses down there right now, and one of the judge's staff went to inform the sheriff. Roark, would you be able to stay here with Jennifer and the children today?"

"Because of the planned touring around, that was already a part of my day, Chance. I'll keep this house locked tight. Will you be gone long?"

"Your description of that blanket coat nudged a little memory, Roark. I'm going to have a talk with a couple of people and will be back just as soon as I can. Don't let anyone in except me, Hawkeye, or the judge. Jenny, did you bring that Colt you like so much?"

"You bet I did, Chance," she said. "I'll keep it close. You find that man, Jacob Chance, and you beat the tar out of him. You bring him back here and I'll beat the tar out of him, too. How dare he," she said. "You get him."

Chance was still chuckling when he mounted his big Morgan stud and rode back into Carson City proper, and found Hawkeye Byrnes talking with a deputy. The snow was piling up, the cold had turned dangerous, and a blizzard was the order of the day.

"Did anyone come up with a description?" Chance asked, stepping off his big horse.

"Only thing I got was the guy was wearing a blanket coat. I guess that's a bit unusual around these parts," he said. "Just a thin cowboy, nothing special except the blanket coat. With the weather, he kept his head down, and the hood from the coat was pulled up. Nobody recognized the man."

"Mean anything to you, deputy?" Chance didn't have much confidence in the sheriff's people, but he had to ask.

"Not much to go on, marshal. A bay horse and a blanket coat, doesn't give you much to go on." The deputy shrugged his shoulders and walked off, figuring the matter closed.

Chance stood shaking his head, slowly, and watched the man walk away. "There goes a real law dog, Hawkeye," he spat out. "I don't think he knows a crime was committed. What is it about that blanket coat that keeps nagging at me? We've seen one recently, Hawkeye, but I can't remember where."

"There was one hanging near the fireplace at Carrington's, Chance. The rifle was standing in that rack and the coat was hanging above it. And, I'm pretty sure it had fringes along the sleeves."

"You're right, Byrnes, it was right there. I wonder if Carrington's foreman decided he might like it since the boss won't be back for a while." He chuckled. "Let's ride, compadre, hard and fast."

***

On the south edge of Carson City, at a small and dirty little saloon that catered to every card shark and confidence man in Nevada, sat Seamus O'Brien and Thomas Bigler, wondering if anything else could possibly go wrong with their plans or their lives. "I saw the whole thing, Seamus. Oscar tried to snatch that kid, the big guy grabbed the kid, and Oscar rode out of town waving the kid's jacket.

"The funny thing, I thought, was Oscar was wearing Carrington's prized blanket coat. Stood out like a beacon, I'll tell you." Thomas Bigler supported what Burleson and O'Brien were working toward, but had not been part of much of the planning, and wasn't aware that the kid he was talking about was Marshal Jacob Chance's son.

"I don't know who the bigger fool is," O'Brien snarled. "Me for offering Oscar the job, or Oscar for taking it. That marshal will find out about that coat, will zero in on Oscar, and he will simply tell the marshal all about me." One more failed plot and O'Brien wasn't aware that he was doomed. "I've got to find Oscar before that marshal does, and kill him dead."

"What can we do?" Bigler asked. "I'm told that Spencer's man, Whistler, told the marshal all about our plans, about our payments to the legislature, and about our attempts on Stanfield's life. He's already got our names and what we've been attempting. I'm pulling out, Seamus. My son can run my ranch. He owns it lock, stock and barrel, Seamus, and I'm heading for Texas."

"If I was smart, I would too," O'Brien all but whispered. The longer he sat at the table with Bigler, the angrier he got. The more he drank, the more he was sure he had to kill Oscar very soon. It was at least a half hour after Bigler left that O'Brien finally picked up and walked out the door, furious that Oscar didn't nab the boy, even more angry that he wore that blanket coat.

"I gotta kill that stupid sumbitch," he said again and again through an alcoholic haze.

Chapter Seventeen

Nate Burleson stepped off his horse, tied it to the rack, and strolled into the Silver Star Saloon, hoping to have a chat with Dirty Dick Robinette. He had spent more than a full day wondering just how he and O'Brien were going to get out of the problem that Henry Carrington was now facing. Carrington knew everything, and Burleson was also aware that Ted Whistler had provided most of what Spencer knew and how the plans were operated.

"I'm looking at two huge problems right now," he muttered more than once on the ride into town. "How to find a way to get out of this, that's problem number one. Finding that way. Will I be able to save my ranch? Maybe there's a third question that needs to be answered. Which is more important?" He found himself angry at Carrington, angry at O'Brien, and yet, he continued to justify his own involvement.

Too many people knew everything there was to know about the bribe money passed to members of the legislature and about the plans to kill Amos Stanfield, and Burleson couldn't come up with a plan to save his hide. It was much more than hide he needed to save, it was a well-producing ranch and lots of money that were in jeopardy.

Burleson was self-centered in every aspect of his life, only thinking of himself, rarely seeing a larger picture. The idea of killing someone in order to get his way was justification enough, the concept of protecting what he owned by any means, including murder, was also fully justified, simply because it was his. Legal or illegal, moral or immoral, were questions that other men might face, but not Nate Burleson. His only thought on the matter wasn't a question, rather a statement: *It's mine, therefore it's right.*

"Bigler has family, at least a son, but I don't, and I'm not willing to give that ranch up. If I can make it look like I sold the ranch, then I can get away and still get all the benefits." He could not come up with a single person that he knew he could trust with that kind of a scam. "Sure as hell couldn't make that kind of arrangement with my foreman or any of the hands."

The group had dealt with Spencer and Dirty Dick for so long, that Burleson simply turned to Robinette, despite the fact that he had never come up with a single productive solution. "Give me a whiskey," he said, sliding up to the half-filled bar. "Where's Dirty Dick?"

"He ain't with us no more, Burleson," the barman answered, putting a bottle and glass in front of the rancher. "Got hisself kilt, he did."

"Dead? Dirty Dick Robinette is dead? How did that happen?"

"Seamus O'Brien come in here early yestiddy mornin' and stomped him to death," the barman said. "It was ugly, what I heard. Stomped his head till he died, and then just walked on out. Wasn't here, myself, but that's what old Twimble done been tellin'."

"Did they arrest O'Brien?" Burleson asked, wondering just what else might go wrong around his life.

"Naw, deputy figgered it was self-defense," and he laughed through a deep cough, almost slapping the bar, it was so funny to think on. "Dirty Dick attacking Seamus O'Brien? Sure, an' maybe that mouse did attack an elephant," and he continued his almost hysterical laughing.

Burleson poured two quick drinks, standing in almost amazement, wondering how all this could be happening to him. His thoughts were interrupted by a deputy walking into the saloon and ordering a beer. "Drinkin' on duty, are we?" Burleson asked, a certain tone to his voice.

"After what just happened, I think I need one," Deputy Gerald Olsen said, taking his pint half down in one swallow. "Damnedest thing you ever saw, Burleson. A cowboy just came swooping down at a full gallop and tried to snatch Marshal Chance's son right off the street."

"What?" Burleson wailed his question. "Say that again."

"Just what I said, Burleson. Cowboy rode up fast, grabbed the boy, but somebody else grabbed the boy and all that cowboy got was the kid's jacket, which he rode out of town still holding. Never seen anything like that, ever."

"You're sure it was the marshal's kid? My God." Burleson's mind was flooded with a visual of the scene, and he wanted to retch, wanted to run, flee, and knew that he had nowhere to go.

"Yeah, the marshal's wife and the children were in a buggy, and were stopping at the little café just down from the Capitol. Marshal Chance was on the scene in just minutes. The funny thing was, that cowboy was wearin' a blanket coat. Not many of them around this country."

Burleson's eyes widened at that, and he knew what had happened. *O'Brien must have hired Carrington's foreman to snatch the kid, and the fool must have worn that coat that Henry liked so much. Damn fools, that's what we've been dealing with. Fools.*

"You didn't give chase? You didn't recognize the man? What's the sheriff going to do?" Burleson had millions of questions, some of which could not be asked.

"My horse was too far away for me to try to chase the fool, and he didn't get the kid, so he was safe. Don't know if the sheriff even knows about it," the deputy said. Burleson didn't understand why the deputy was in the saloon instead of dealing with the crime at hand, but knew he had to find O'Brien before his world collapsed on him.

The deputy had one more beer and Burleson had two more whiskies, and they left the saloon. "You keeping Carrington at what's left of the jail?" Burleson asked.

"No. Marshal Chance has him locked up at the state prison along with Smith and Sammy Lauck. Hell, we ain't got a single cell left," he joked, walking up the street. Burleson mounted his horse and started the long ride to his ranch, wondering just how long it would be before Chance paid him a visit.

The weather had taken a decided move toward becoming a major storm as he rode out of town. The wind was blowing hard out of the north, and what had been a light snow falling was now heavy snow blowing about, creating drifts and obscuring vision. "I feel as cold and bleak as this storm," he muttered, kicking his horse into a lope, racing to find O'Brien and find out if he was behind the kidnap attempt.

***

"These men are getting desperate, Hawkeye," Chance said, as they rode through the heavy wet snow toward the Carrington spread. The weather simply wouldn't let up, storm after storm blowing down from the northwest, covering the Sierra Nevada with as much as twenty feet at the highest elevations. With this new one, there was close to a foot of snow on the valley floor, and what was falling was cold and sopping wet.

"They aren't working from a plan now," Chance continued. "Their power plays failed, their assassination attempts failed, and now they are reacting, not thinking, and we are going to be facing the most dangerous type of man, the caged, frightened, pitiful criminal with nowhere to go."

"You don't believe that feller that tried to kidnap Little Jake was one of them, do you?"

"No, he was just another hired gun. I'm betting it was that foreman at Carrington's. Either Burleson or O'Brien, or both, got to him with a handful of gold coins, and no plan. Here's a bet for you, Hawkeye." He smiled and chuckled at the young man. "When we get there, we'll find a lathered-up horse near the barn, and a blanket coat inside the ranch house, but just flung down on a chair, not hung up nice and pretty."

"The alternative to that, marshal," Hawkeye joshed, "is, we'll not find any horse, and there won't be any coat of any kind in the ranch house. I've got a dollar says I'm right."

They nodded that the bet was down and covered, and continued the ride through the howling blizzard. "I was working a job up in Wyoming country many years ago when a storm like this blew through," Chance reminisced, "and had my stage robbing bandit in custody when we got trapped at a cabin high in the Rocky Mountains. We took turns chopping wood and bringing it in, took turns melting snow for water, even took turns cooking our meals.

"Damn thing was, he knew he couldn't escape, but never once turned on me with the ax or a knife. I put in a good word with the judge and he went straight as an arrow after that. Other men I've run into would have tried to kill me in an instant and still been stuck in the blizzard."

The light banter continued until they rode up to the ranch house and found the door open and the Chinese cook waving to them. "Don't see that lathered up horse, marshal." Byrnes laughed, jumping down from his mount. The two came up on the porch to talk to the excited cook.

"Come, come," the man said, pointing at the fireplace. "All gone."

The rack was still standing but the rifle, the gun belt and revolver, and the blanket coat were no longer there. "Oscar grab, knock me down," the cook tried to get out in his own brand of English, showing a large lump on his jaw where he took a heavy punch. "Maybe one hour."

"With this wet snow," Chance muttered, "there won't be one track to follow, and since he didn't get the job done, he'll be hightailing it out of this country. Whichever of our two suspects hired him is probably angry enough to shoot the man if he tried to make contact. Let's ride by O'Brien's and see if our friendly killer is out and about."

"Somebody has to take possession of this ranch, Chance. I doubt that cook has any idea that Carrington won't be coming home, and the cattle and animals won't have someone caring for them."

"According to Elmer Barlow, the Douglas County sheriff has been alerted and will send someone out. No bets on that one," he chuckled.

***

Burleson changed his mind about O'Brien, partly because of the storm, but mostly because he wanted to be safe himself, save his ranch, save his money. He rode quietly back to his ranch, slowly putting together an idea that might get him out of this country and save his ranch as well. "If I sell it to Micah Doyle with a written agreement that he is just running it for me, and when the time comes, he can sell it for true, I'll get my money. Whatever he makes while he's running the ranch, we'll split."

Doyle was a money grubber at best, but would he really take such deal? Burleson's selfishness and denial of the situation was obvious but most would concede that Doyle wasn't smart enough to see the problem.

Burleson, O'Brien, Carrington, and Bigler had been making regular payments to Doyle for several years, which allowed them to run their operations any way they wanted, allowed them to hire wanted men from time to time to get their way or else, and allowed for some shady brand work on range animals to the south and east of the valley. The

Washoe Tribe of Indians lost considerable numbers of calves every spring, and Doyle simply suggested a large coyote and wolf population was working the eastern slope of the Sierra range.

All of the ranches were in Douglas County and none of the illegal or questionable acts took place in that county, thus Douglas County wasn't even aware of a problem. Before Stanfield's attempted assassination, even the state's attorney general wasn't aware there was a problem. Burleson and company's plans weren't understood at all by Doyle.

Burleson's plan would just be one more step down the ladder for Doyle. Doyle had the word of the group that they would give full political backing for whatever the criminal sheriff wanted to do. Doyle would seem to be a successful rancher and would take that next step toward the governor's office. All those thoughts were roaming through Burleson's mind as he turned his horse toward his ranch house, and came up short, seeing O'Brien's horse tethered there.

"I heard some bad things when I was in town, Seamus," he said, walking into the ranch house and finding O'Brien standing near the fireplace. "Just what have you done? They told me you killed Dirty Dick Robinette, and then I heard that Carrington's been arrested, and then I heard that Carrington's foreman tried to kidnap Marshal Chance's kid. Have you lost your mind?"

"Don't you ever talk to me that way, Burleson," O'Brien said, stepping toward the rancher and planting a big fist square on the man's nose, sending him backward and right out the door, where he landed with a splash in the heavy wet snow and mud. Seamus O'Brien took three quick steps through the door and was about to plant a boot in Burleson's face when a gunshot went off, and a bullet sprayed wood chips into O'Brien's face, stopping the man cold.

Burleson had a smoking Colt revolver in his hand, aimed at O'Brien's groin, and a nasty look on his face. "You might get away with that with some people, Seamus, but not with me," and he moved the pistol slightly upward, firing a shot that whistled past O'Brien's ear, making the man jump back inside the house, trying to get his heavy winter coat opened. "That piece hanging on your hip is useless if you can't get at it, Seamus. Sit down, and tell me what the hell you've done."

O'Brien did what he was told, and Burleson, still holding the gun in the most threatening manner, sat in a chair across from him. "We're going to have attorney general investigators, U.S. marshals, maybe even the damn army down on us, you fool. What have you done?"

"I rode over here to tell you I'm through, Burleson. I'm pulling out, and if I were you, I would too. It's over." O'Brien's fabled temper had been cooled by the two gunshots, and the reality of what was happening.

"There's certainly no doubt about that," Burleson said. "As soon as that fool touched the marshal's kid, it was over." *I had it almost figured out, and now, I'm going to lose everything I've ever worked for. Maybe Carrington was right, maybe all we had to do was offer more money to Stanfield.* He looked into O'Brien's face and saw nothing but anger and fear. "Where would you go, Seamus? You can't run to the west, they'll have every town filled with your picture and the big words, Wanted, Dead or Alive.

"You can't go east, north, or south for the same reason. Spencer's papers that Whistler gave to Chance, Smith's talking a mile a minute at the state prison, and now Carrington jabbering right alongside, was enough to hang us, O'Brien, and now you've killed Dirty Dick Robinette and hired a man to kidnap the marshal's kid. We have no place to run."

Burleson stood up and walked to a cabinet along the wall near the fireplace and brought a bottle of whiskey and two glasses back, and sat down. He poured them each a full glass of fine Kentucky bourbon, offered O'Brien a cigar and lit one for himself, and sat back, glaring at the Irish rancher with the flaming temper. "Drink your drink and leave, Seamus. I don't ever want to see you again."

Burleson never changed where his revolver was pointing, never let his mind wander from the thought, *How do I get out of this alive?* When they were working toward the same goal, he and O'Brien were tight, but now, Burleson was looking at someone trying to take something from him. *I won't lose my freedom or my ranch because of you,* he said to himself, over and over.

O'Brien had hate written across his face, his eyes narrowed to kill, his mouth more grim than Burleson had ever seen. He tipped the glass back and drank it empty, stood, glared some more, and walked out the door, got on his horse, and rode away.

"I might still be able to pull this off if I can get to Micah Doyle before Chance finds me," Burleson murmured, taking his bottle and glass into his office just off the main room. He opened his safe and brought out a large leather pouch that was filled with bills and stamped ingots of gold. He figured there was close to thirty pounds of pure gold along with twenty thousand dollars in large bills.

It was less than an hour later, with a small pack behind his saddle, and the saddlebags filled with the contents of that leather pouch, that Burleson began his long ride back to Carson City and a meeting with Micah Doyle. The weather had grown colder, and the snow, so wet before, was now falling in large fluffy flakes, while the stuff already on the ground was freezing solid.

Chapter Eighteen

"The last time I was this cold," Chance said, "I was riding with an Indian named Eyes Like Cougar, bringing the body of my brother-in-law back to an army fort, and Cougar killed an Arctic hare that we roasted. We could use that rabbit right now." He laughed, as he and Hawkeye Byrnes rode through the open plain of the Carson Valley, used the Cradelbaugh crossing, making their way toward Seamus O'Brien's ranch.

"I've heard stories of men killing buffalo during storms like this and getting inside the body to stay alive. We might have to kill a steer or two, Chance." Byrnes chuckled. "What's our plan if we find O'Brien?"

"I have the arrest warrant from Barlow with me, and even if I didn't, we have the information on the murder of Robinette. Everything I've heard, we better make sure we're ready for a fight if we find him. He's a mean one, Byrnes, and he has a flint strike temper."

"I never had dealings with him, but stories did float up to the Comstock from time to time. Something that's been bothering me is all these jurisdiction problems. In my mind, it seems some people aren't responding as they should. Micah Doyle is Ormsby County sheriff and operates out of Carson City, the county seat, but all the ranchers involved in the conspiracy live here in the Carson Valley, which is in Douglas County. Is the Douglas County sheriff even aware of our investigation?"

He stopped short and pulled his horse to a stop, pointing off in the distance. "Hard to see with all this snow, Chance, but is that a man riding hard toward the ranch?"

Chance held his arm up, trying to fend off some of the wind whipped flakes, and nodded. "I think so," he said.

"That might be O'Brien, and that is his ranch right in front of us. Let's ride in a little faster, Mr. Byrnes," he said, nudging the big Morgan into a trot. "Maybe we can catch him unawares, but be ready for a fight." The snow had been coming down for several hours and the wind had built drifts higher than a standing man.

The horses were doing as much plowing as they were trying to run. "I don't think he's spotted us yet, Chance," Byrnes hollered. "I don't think these horses have much left in them, either. If he makes a break, I don't know if we will be able to chase him." Chance just growled his answer, which amounted to a guttural "Yup."

O'Brien rode hard through the storm on the long ride across the Carson Valley and as he turned into the lane leading to his ranch house he spotted two riders coming toward him at a fast trot. "Sumbitch," he snarled, kicking his horse into a full gallop, reining to a stop at the ranch porch and jumping from the saddle. He ran for the door, trying to open his heavy winter coat, and hit a patch of ice that dumped him in a heap at the door.

Chance and Byrnes bailed off their horses, as O'Brien tried to recover from the fall, and raced toward the porch. Chance had his rifle in hand and Byrnes had a handful of cold Colt steel, ready to shoot in an instant. O'Bricn was still fumbling with his coat when Chance stuck the rifle in his chest. "Stop!" is all he needed to say, and O'Brien slumped onto the icy porch.

***

After a long hour's discussion spent in the living room at the O'Brien ranch, with a fire raging in the fireplace, and mugs of steaming coffee consumed, Chance was ready to bring O'Brien back to Carson City. "I won't put up with any problem, O'Brien. You will be in restraints and you will come with us, now," he said, pulling a set of handcuffs from his heavy bearskin coat.

O'Brien started to growl his answer but Hawkeye Byrnes was standing in front of him with his revolver in hand. "Just put your hands behind your back, O'Brien," Byrnes said, quietly. "Is there someone here who can take care of the place?" O'Brien didn't answer and Chance gave him a nudge.

"Hands behind your back." Byrnes snarled it out this time. O'Brien spun around and smacked Chance with his massive left fist, knocking the marshal back several feet, but not down. Chance got his feet set and lunged at the big rancher, driving him across the living room and into the wall, knocking the breath out of the man.

O'Brien was strong and recovered quickly, driving a fist into Chance's midsection and following up with a hard fist to his jaw. O'Brien was about to follow up when Byrnes fired a shot into the wall, very close to the Irishman's head. The fight was over and Chance, bleeding from a cut lip, whipped O'Brien around and cranked the cuffs down hard.

"It's time for you to learn some manners, Mr. O'Brien," Chance snarled, shoving the man out the door and into the face of the blizzard. "Let's get this fool back to Carson City and into a cold damn jail cell, Mr. Byrnes."

"I'm all in favor of taking him the way he is, marshal, but we don't want to bring a dead man in. Let's get him in his winter coat." He chuckled, and Chance, too, laughed just a little bit. They were in the saddle in moments and on their way.

"I knew I should have just shot you, O'Brien," Byrnes said. "That way we could have sat in front of your fire for another hour or so. Can I just go ahead and shoot him, marshal?"

"No, not yet, Hawkeye. We'll let him steam some, get good and angry, and maybe the fool will make a break for it. You gonna run, Irish?

"In answer to your other question, Hawkeye," Chance said after all the chuckles, "I doubt that Doyle even recognized the threat to Stanfield or the conspiracy until we laid it on his desk, and there is no reason for the Douglas County sheriff to know anything about any of it.

"I was amazed that the attorney general was clueless." He chortled through an icy moustache. "It seems the higher up the political or social ladder a person might be the less likely it is that they will be thought to be criminal. These men are very wealthy land owners with large herds of fine cattle, and in many minds that kind of person certainly can't be considered a criminal."

"Hah!" is all Byrnes said, and they continued plodding their way through deep drifts of gale-blown snow, coming into the capital city several hours later. "Let's put this fine gentleman up at the state prison, Mr. Byrnes, and then let's find a barrel of boiling coffee."

***

It was dark by the time Chance found his way to his new home and the warmth of a fine fire. "You must be frozen," Jennifer said, taking his ice-covered coat and walking him to the fireplace. "I'll get you a cup of coffee with a hefty dose of brandy in it." She smiled, heading for the kitchen.

"Is Little Jake okay?" Chance asked immediately. "He must have been frightened out of his mind. I never should have brought all of you here. Please don't hate me for what happened, Jenny. I'm sorry."

"Nonsense," she said in as close to a growl as Jennifer could get. "We agreed, and it was I that was completely in favor of the trip. They could just as easily have tried to kidnap one of us while we were in Preston, Jacob." She brought his coffee out and he was glad that it was about half brandy. The fire was more than toasty and the brandy brought the warm blood right up to the surface quickly.

"Tell me about this whole affair, Chance," she said, settling into a large overstuffed armchair near the fire. "It's so confusing to me. I'll have supper ready in just a few minutes. The children and I ate hours ago. Amos had Augie Roark brought over a large leg of lamb and it's in the oven, warming now. Is Amos going to be okay? I don't know whether to be worried or not, Chance."

"I think it's safe to say that any threats that might have been are gone now," Chance said, bending over and giving her a warm, brandy infused kiss. "There're at least one or two more individuals that Byrnes and I have to find, and I'm sure we will. They don't pose any kind of threat and are probably making plans to get out of this area as quickly as possible.

"You're all safe, the judge is safe, and right now the conspiracy is broken. The fallout will be fun to watch when Barlow starts issuing arrest warrants for many of the lawmakers who will be arriving for the new legislative session. For public officials of their standing to be accused of open bribery is damn serious." He chuckled. "I saw Jerrod Stockton earlier this morning and he delivered all those letters and notes to Barlow. Those same letters were offers of money and property in exchange for votes in favor of specific legislation, and Stockton had all the names of the men that responded in favor.

"There will be some empty seats as they convene next week," he said. He finished his coffee, stuffed more wood in the fire and stood, with just the hint of a smile on his rugged face. "I have to admit it felt good putting the iron to those men's wrists, but I'll sure be glad when this is over. I'm just getting a little old for this game, Jenny."

"You won't be old when you're ninety, Jacob Chance, you've just discovered the good life of ranching and being married to the most wonderful girl in the world." She was laughing and dancing and he grabbed her, pulled her close and gave her a long, wet kiss, all the time patting her little bottom end. "I do love you, Marshal Chance."

***

"What the hell are you doing here?" Sheriff Micah Doyle said, holding the door to his home open for Nate Burleson. "Come in, man, damn but you look frozen solid. Come in, stand by the fire, let me get you a drink."

It was late in the evening by the time Burleson had made it to the sheriff's home and he was frozen to the bone, almost incoherent, accepting the glass of whiskey from Doyle. It was several minutes before he was thawed out enough to make himself understood. "It's all over, Micah. Our fight is finished. Carrington is in prison, O'Brien is running away, Bigler is running away, and I have a plan that will let me get out alive, too."

"From what I'm hearing, you'll be lucky to end up alive, not get away," Doyle said, pouring another glass of whiskey for each of them. "Marshal Chance and young Hawkeye Byrnes are working for Barlow and have arrest warrants for you and many others. You're certainly right, though. It's over. Amos Stanfield will publish the majority opinion tomorrow, and Nevada's water laws will be on the books."

"Here's my plan, Micah," Burleson said, and the two sat down across from each other at a large table.

Chapter Nineteen

It was another full day before the storm broke and life in the capital city returned to its normal state of chaos, legislators and their family and staff pouring in from all over the state, railroad crews keeping the lines open despite tons of drifted snow, and crews continuing to build the rails north toward Reno, and surveying the route south that would serve Minden.

"There's no reason for me to be nervous, I'm only a spectator," Elaine Stockton said, adjusting her hat for the tenth time that evening. It was a grand occasion, the opening of the new legislature with Nevada's new governor, Lewis R. Bradley, doing the honors. Bradley was the first democrat elected governor of the new state, and he and his lieutenant governor, Frank Denver, were in their most elegant dress.

Even the weather seemed to be in a festive mood, with clear, cold skies sprinkled generously with brilliantly shining stars. Winds in western Nevada can be devastating, and on this night were very calm. The first of the miners to rush to the Comstock had jokingly referred to the blasting winds as Washoe Zephyrs.

"You're more than a spectator, Elaine," Jenny Chance said, "you're Senator Jerrod Stockton's wife. And just look at him. Where on earth were you able to find formal wear for a man of his size?"

"I couldn't." She tinkled in her softest laugh. "I had to make it myself. They don't make clothing for a man that big. I make all his clothes or he'd be dressed in feed sacks."

Senator Stockton just harrumphed and suggested that it wouldn't be proper to be late for the governor's speech, and everyone slowly made their way to carriages.

Amos Stanfield in his judicial robes and his law clerk, Augustus (Augie) Roark, in formal wear, escorted by two armed outriders, rode in one carriage, Jacob and Jennie Chance with Senator and Mrs. Stockton in another. "My goodness, Chance, I'm as nervous as Elaine," Jenny said, snuggling as close to him as she could get.

"It's been many years since I've dressed like this." Chance chuckled, sticking a finger inside his stiff collar, moving his head around a bit. "It isn't something I would want to do on a regular basis."

"Did young Slim Crockett get out of town okay?" Jerrod asked as the carriage began its short journey to the Capitol building. "I know he was sure anxious."

Chance laughed. "I've never seen a boy so willing to get out of Carson City. He spent half a day in Virginia City, rode up and back in one day, and was on his way back to Preston the next morning. I think Roger Bullis will be conducting his first marriage ceremony for his daughter Clementine very soon, Jerrod."

As they pulled up to the Capitol building and stepped out of the carriage, Attorney General Elmer Barlow drove up. "General Barlow, it's good to see you," Chance said, extending his hand. "My dear wife, Jennifer, I believe you know Senator Stockton and his wife, Elaine."

"Chance, I can't thank you enough for busting up that conspiracy to murder our friend Justice Stanfield. Splendid work, sir. Will we ever be able to find Nate Burleson?"

"That's an under the table deal he made with Doyle. I arrested Doyle this afternoon for aiding and abetting. Hawkeye arrested Bigler's son on the same charges. You'll find all the paperwork on your desk in the morning.

"Hawkeye thinks he knows where Burleson might try to make his way out of here and is on his way now. He had provisions for a week, so we'll just have to wait. I got a telegram from the sheriff in Winnemucca. They picked up Bigler at the train station, trying to buy a ticket to Chicago.

"All in all, general, I think we did pretty well for ourselves."

"You did splendid, Marshal Chance, splendid."

***

The evening was formal from beginning to end, with speeches made by everyone who had ever wanted to make a speech, Jenny thought, and she had to nudge Chance more than once to keep him from snoring too loud. The evening finally ended with Governor Bradley declaring the legislature open for the session, and everyone headed to either parties or gatherings.

Amos Stanfield held a small dinner party at his home, and many hours later Jenny and Chance managed to get next door and into the warmth of their abode. "No talk, no drinks, no coffee, just a warm bed and you," Chance said as they came in. Throwing off overcoats and jackets, hats and wraps, shoes and boots, the two slipped into their upstairs bedroom and peace and quiet.

"I really enjoyed seeing all those empty seats on the floor of the legislature," Chance said. "We did our job."

"You did your job, Marshal Chance. Amos Stanfield would be a dead man right now if it weren't for you."

***

They all try to do the same thing, and believe they are the first to think of it. Hawkeye laughed to himself, riding his high stepping Arab stud and trailing a mule packed for a long trip through the Nevada desert in the middle of winter. *Hide out in a little town where no one knows you, and then, in a few weeks, make your real break for freedom. I'll have Burleson in irons before the week is out.*

Hawkeye Byrnes had been sheriff in Virginia City for several years and western Nevada's little mining communities were well known to him. One such town was Aurora in the mountains in Esmeralda County. It was a thriving mining town a few years before but was on the decline. *Burleson thinks he's pretty smart, and he surely does know this country, but I'll bet he's heard all the stories about Aurora.*

It'll take me two days to get there, one day to find that fool, and two days to bring him back to Carson City. He had brought more than one citizen of the Comstock back from the bowels of Aurora, and knew the trail. He skirted Walker Lake and made the long push into the high mountains.

It was a steep climb to what they called Lucky Boy Pass and then across the range and into Aurora. The winter had brought several major storms and the snow pack at the high elevations was deep. On top of that, Byrnes had elected to take what he considered a shorter passage but on a less used trail.

"Snow is thick here, maybe I should have come in from the Mono trail," he muttered, plowing through snow that hadn't welcomed a visitor in weeks. He stopped twice to make sure the wraps he had on his horse's legs were holding, that ice wasn't slicing into the legs. "If Burleson tried to get to Aurora, he went the other way," he snarled.

Byrnes made a cold camp that first night, mostly to punish himself for being headstrong about taking the shorter route, but changed his mind in the morning, and with the temperature well below the zero mark, lit a big fire and ate a big hot breakfast. "All right, Mr. Know-it-all, let's set that head back on straight and start thinking like the man I know I am." He cussed himself through most of the day, fighting through heavy drifts of snow, almost losing the trail more than once.

Criminals liked to try to hide out in Aurora for two reasons. The citizenry weren't particularly offended by their presence, and both Nevada and California claimed the little town. There was an Esmeralda County sheriff's deputy and a deputy from California's Mono County, supervisors from both states, and opposing laws from the two states. It was assumed, then, that no one knew who had jurisdiction, and therefore, no one did. It was often described as a lawless little mining town.

Burleson's plans were simple, to remain in Aurora for two, maybe three weeks, until he figured most of the heat would be off, then he would ride south through the long and beautiful Owens Valley and into the Los Angeles basin, or maybe turn southeast and make his way to New Mexico or Texas. "That fool Micah Doyle will work my ranch, raise my cattle, and send me money at every sale. I'll come back in a couple of years, throw the fool out, and retake what's mine."

He took a hotel room, was very careful not to flash his money about, and settled in, letting those few he met understand that he might be interested in investing in one of the local mining properties, or maybe a saloon, or possibly a hotel. He dressed as a prosperous rancher, which he was, ate at the finest restaurant, and drank at the gilded Aurora Beacon saloon and dancehall.

His hotel was on Pine Street, near the corner of Silver Street, while the saloon and some of the bawdy houses were located along Antelope Street, which incidentally was also Mono Creek during heavy rains and spring runoff.

There were many in Aurora who wanted to have the pleasure of Mr. Evan Banter's company, and possibly sell him some prime property. Aurora's mines by this time were beginning to slow down, ore grades were low, and many were thinking of selling and moving out.

"Mr. Banter." Benjamin Templeton smiled, offering a cigar. "I've heard of your ranching operation in Elko. There are some fine properties here in Aurora, not ranching of course, but good mining prospects." Burleson laughed to himself at that, knowing he couldn't possibly have any ranches in Elko since the man Banter didn't even exist.

"I'm sure there are, Templeton, but tonight I'd much rather think about the prospects of spending some time at that gambling table over there." Burleson picked up his snifter of brandy and strolled across the saloon toward the gambling den in the back, taking an empty chair.

"Table stakes, is it?" he asked, slipping a few of those large bills from his engraved leather purse. He played the most conservative hands of poker in his life, watching the dealer palm cards, slip cards, fake shuffling too. After the dealer drew two hands in a row of four aces king high, he picked up his money and said goodnight.

***

It was very late that night when a lone rider and pack mule came into town, and made arrangements with the livery operator for the animals and a little extra room for one tired Nevada State attorney general deputy inspector to flop his bedroll. "It is cold up in these hills," he said through chattering teeth. "Wouldn't have some coffee tucked in that little office, would you?"

The stable hand was still shaking off the deep sleep that was interrupted by Byrnes' arrival. "Now I recognize you, Hawkeye. What the hell are you doing in this miserable excuse for a town?"

Hawkeye Byrnes stood stock still for a full minute giving the big man a long look, top to bottom. Lawmen never know when they might run into someone with whom they may have had previous history. Hawkeye was still in his buffalo robe long coat, cinched tight, and would never have been able to reach a weapon if it was needed.

It took a long moment before he thought he recognized the man behind the voice. "Is it Isaac Powell? I wondered where you wandered off to. It's been two years, Ike. How are you? All healed up?"

Ike Powell had been in a big mine accident at the Yellow Jacket Mine on the Comstock, had helped save many members of his crew, but was busted up something fierce in the fire and cave-in. Many of the miners had not been so lucky in the tragedy. "I don't move like I did, Hawkeye, and I ain't been underground a day since, but I'm making out.

"Bought into this operation and run a string of mules, too. This ain't the kind of weather a man should find himself in." He gave a little twist to his head, asking the question without using words. Powell was a wise man, well read, a leader at the Yellow Jacket, and Hawkeye felt he now had a friend and probably back up, if he needed it, to bring Burleson in.

"I'm working for the attorney general, Ike, and I'm trailing a man wanted for numerous crimes. His name's Nate Burleson, but I'm sure he isn't calling himself that, right now. He's a hefty man, probably forties, and a rancher. Mean anything to you?"

"Yup," Ike Powell said, ushering him into his little office where the potbelly stove was bright red and the coffee was boiling. "But first though, which attorney general?"

Hawkeye laughed a good one at that. "Nevada, my friend, Nevada. You think they'll ever get that figured out? Town can't be in two states at the same time, just can't."

"Esmeralda Deputy Swan got in a fist fight with Mono Deputy Tucker the other night, and then they tried to arrest each other. It can be fun up here, Hawkeye, can be. Now, about your man.

"I thought I recognized him when he rode in. He's calling himself Evan Banter, spends his evenings at the Aurora Beacon, and is staying, I think, at the Esmeralda House, on Pine Street. I'm sure it's Burleson. He used to come to Virginia City and try to swagger with John Mackay and Jim Fair. They shucked him off pretty good, if I remember.

"So what did he do to get you off that mountain and working for old Elmer Barlow?"

It took another full pot of coffee for Byrnes to bring Powell up to speed, and the two watched as the sun slowly brought Aurora into the new day. Hawkeye found a room at a dirty little miner's flophouse, slept till noon, and started making his rounds of the town. "I've been here many times, but it's always best to really know where things are and find out if there have been any changes," he mumbled, stopping first at the Millionaire's Club, a saloon with high thoughts of itself. It advertised a free lunch and ten cent beer.

"Can't beat a deal like this," he said with a chuckle to the barman. Great slabs of roast venison, sausages steamed in beer, and fried pork cracklins filled his platter, and he joshed with the barman that it would take at least three beers to get it all washed down. He settled up with the barman, tucked a couple of cigars in his pocket and lit another, and had started toward the batwings when he spotted Burleson walking on the other side of the street.

Antelope Street, along with numerous saloons and gambling parlors, featured some of the better things in life, such as two bath houses, barber shops, and a couple of cobbler's shops.

Byrnes stood to the side, in the shadows, and watched Burleson step into one of the barbershops. The sign proclaimed hot baths, full tonsorial services, and dentistry. Byrnes slipped across the street and waited about ten minutes before he made his move for the shop. He opened the great buffalo robe coat, made sure his badge was very obvious and his revolver was available, and stepped into the barbershop, which was empty except for the barber.

"A tall, husky gentleman stepped into this fine parlor a few minutes ago, Barber. Where might I find him?" Hawkeye Byrnes said with a smile.

The barber saw the badge, saw the glint in Byrnes' eye, and noticed how close Byrnes' hand was to his weapon. He nodded toward a curtain and almost whispered, "He's having a hot bath, sir."

Byrnes gave a nod back to the barber, suggested that he might find it safer out on the street, pulled his revolver and stepped through the curtains. A charmingly lovely Chinese woman, stark naked, was in the tub with Burleson, whose back was toward the curtains. She saw Hawkeye, saw the barrel end of that revolver pointed at her and screamed, jumped from the tub, slipped on the wet floor and went down hard.

Burleson whipped around, tried to reach his holstered weapon on the rack near the tub, and Byrnes simply said, "No!" Byrnes moved around to face the hefty rancher, had his heavy revolver cocked and pointed at one of Burleson's more tender areas, and said, "You're under arrest, Nate Burleson.

"Get out of the tub, slow now, cuz I really do want to shoot you, and stand over there," and he pointed toward the wall behind the tub. Byrnes grabbed Burleson's pants and holstered weapon, checked the pockets and threw the pants at the man.

He took Burleson's coat off the hook, checked those pockets and threw it at the man, too. The shirt and boots followed, and Burleson slowly got dressed, looking down the barrel of Hawkeye's big, cocked revolver. "Hands behind your back, Burleson," Byrnes said, and clicked the handcuffs into place. He marched the rancher down the main street of Aurora to the Esmeralda County deputy's office and had him locked up.

"Thank you, Deputy Swan. It's too late to start back today. I'll get his things from his hotel room and we'll head back to Carson City at sunrise. All the paperwork's in order and you'll be compensated for his food and lodging by the AG. In fact, if you want, I'll take the chit back with me in the morning."

"I'm sure the county would appreciate that, Hawkeye," Swan said. "It's good to see you again. Just bang on the door in the morning, I'll hear you."

Good to see you again? That man's not been in Virginia City a day in his life. Is every single person in this town playing some kind of game? There's not a straight man in town. He laughed, looking around for the hotel that Burleson was staying at. *I'll pack up his property and have a hot meal somewhere, and be out of this town as early as I possibly can.*

Chapter Twenty

Mid-winter is cold and it gets dark fast in the mountains of western Nevada. It was only four o'clock in the afternoon, but it was already twilight in Aurora. Hawkeye Byrnes decided to stay the night in Burleson's hotel room, since it was already paid for, and he spent a couple of hours packaging Burleson's property for the trip out in the morning. "For a man running away he surely did carry a bunch of stuff," he muttered, rolling up dress pants, jackets, and shirts.

Burleson hadn't held back on his selection of a hotel, and the room featured a large bed with a feather mattress, big fluffy pillows, ample closet space, a writing table and chair, and thick curtains to allow sleeping-in come morning. The carpet was a thick wool blend with a subdued pattern.

"Well, now, look at this would you," Byrnes muttered, opening up a large cigar tin. "No wonder these cigars weigh so much." He emptied the large tin onto the bed and counted out ten bars of gold, each stamped at twelve ounces troy. "Each of these is one pound. Damn fool was running away in style." Each of those one hundred twenty ounces was valued at twenty dollars, Hawkeye knew, and he whistled at what he had found.

"That man was running away in style," he murmured again, and a wicked grin spread across his face. He tucked the bars back into the tin, and put the tin inside one of Burleson's carpetbags. "Good thing I'm a law-abidin' lawman. I'll have to get Powell to help me get all this stuff ready for our trip in the morning. That old mule better eat good tonight." He chuckled, heading out of the hotel for the stables.

"It's gonna be a miserable ride back unless I can talk old Mr. Powell into joining me on the trail. Burleson's a big husky rancher and I can't keep his hands cuffed behind his back for two full days. Maybe tie him to a tree overnight?" He had to laugh at that thought, but he knew the dangers of transporting big strong prisoners over long distances alone.

"See you got your man, Hawkeye. From the talk around town, that little Chinese girl wet her pants for ten minutes when you appeared with that cannon you carry."

He chuckled. "She didn't do that, Ike. She couldn't do that. She wasn't wearing any pants. Neither was Burleson. I gave thought to marching him to jail in his altogether, but didn't do that. Coffee hot?"

"Come on in and tell me your plans," Powell said.

"I want to leave out as close to sunrise as I can, get out of these mountains and make the second day's ride much shorter, but I'm pretty sure I need help, Ike. My mule will be carrying an oversize pack and I'll be alone with a big prisoner." He took a long drink of hot coffee and refilled his cup. "When was the last time you were in the capital?"

"Subtle, that's old Hawkeye Byrnes." Ike Powell laughed. "Might be good for me to get away for a few days. Pete Jackson can run this place. I've got Burleson's horse in a stall back there, so he'd be set, and I'll pack your mule and another, give 'em both light loads, and be ready at sunrise, Mr. Byrnes."

"Good, Ike, good. I'll see you in the morning. Whatever you need to buy, get receipts so you can be reimbursed by the AG," and he left Burleson's gear all bundled and ready to be packed.

He had a good feeling about the trip back, having good company along with that extra protection. "We will definitely take the Mono road out of here, and then head north, and we'll be on well-travelled roads the whole way."

He snickered, still kicking himself for taking the short route up the mountain. "I've had a good day," he said quietly. "I think I'll let General Barlow buy me a big steak, mashed potatoes, and hot apple pie for supper. Yes, I will."

***

"Get me out of here, Swan. I've got gold, I can make it right with you. You don't need to carry a bent up old tin badge for the rest of your life. Let me out, I've got a box full of gold, we can ride for Owens Valley and be in Arizona in two days." Burleson was pleading with the Esmeralda County deputy and getting nowhere.

"You trying to bribe a lawman is just gonna get you a bunch more years in prison, old man. Don't bring it up again." Swan walked into the front of the office and out the door, heading for the Aurora Beacon Saloon and a cold beer. *He said a whole box full of gold*, he all but whispered, walking in the brisk evening air. *I wonder just how big a box he was talking about?* and the gentle chuckle came easy.

"There you are, Hawkeye," he said, coming through the batwings of the saloon. "What's your plan for the morning? By the way, your prisoner offered me a part of what he called a whole box full of gold if I'd let him out. I wanted to ask him how big the box was, but didn't."

"You put that in a report and I'll just add attempted bribery to the long list of charges I'm pressing now. A box of gold, eh? That's interesting." Byrnes wasn't about to tell the deputy or anyone else about a whole cigar tin full of gold. "I want to pick him up at sunrise and be well out of here and out of these mountains before dark."

Swan and Byrnes had another glass of beer together and went their way. Byrnes slipped into the restaurant for supper with plans for an early bedtime and early rise. Swan had pictures of a big box full of gold and slipped into the card room at the back of the saloon and a talk with Ezra

Morrison, called White Beard by his friends. The two sat at a cocktail table for half an hour in deep conversation.

White Beard Morrison wasn't an old man, rather was one of those people whose hair turned white at an early age. In Morrison's case, he found himself mostly bald by the time he was twenty, and what little hair he had was pure white. His beard was white as well, and he wore it full face, long, scraggly. With bright deep brown eyes, he offered a unique look to those around him.

Wanted posters described White Beard Morrison as armed and dangerous, and wanted for stage robbery, bank robbery, murder, and other acts against society. He was never molested by either the Mono deputy or the Esmeralda deputy, and lived a comfortable life in the mining community.

"That's the story, White Beard. Even if it isn't a big box of gold, even if it's a little box of gold, it would be worth it. Byrnes is picking Burleson up at sunrise and if you watch which trail he takes out of town, Walker lake trail or Mono trail, I'll join you and we can ride him down. It would be best if he took the Mono trail. Good places on that trail to jump them."

"With a prisoner and a pack mule, he won't be moving fast," White Beard said, "and we can shadow them until they get in a good place to jump them. Okay, I'll come to the jail as soon as I know which trail they be taking."

Swan headed back to the jail for a plate of beans and biscuits and a long night dreaming about large boxes of gold and a better life in a warmer climate. White Beard Morrison took a place at one of the gambling tables to see if his luck really was turning for the better.

***

"Damn, Ezra, what do you mean you slept in? They've been gone for more than an hour and we don't know which trail they're on." Swan had Burleson up and coffee and cold biscuits in him before Hawkeye Byrnes arrived at sunrise to pick him up, then found himself pacing for more than an hour before White Beard Morrison showed up to say he overslept and had no idea which way they went when they left town.

"We're talking a box of gold you fool," Swan stormed, trying to slip into his heavy winter Mackinaw and wool hat. "Alright, well, let's see what we can find out. Maybe old Jackson saw which way they left." It was a fast and quiet walk down the street to the stables where Pete Jackson was busy cleaning stalls.

"Howdy deputy," he said. "You're up early."

"Want to catch up with that lawman and his prisoner if I can. I have some important information that they need. Did you happen to notice which trail they used to leave town?"

Jackson sucked on an old pipe that hadn't been lit in ages, pushed his hat back a notch, and squinted just one eye. "Contemplatin'," he said. Sucked some more on the pipe, looked out the big barn doors, and finally said, "Yup, sure I am, deputy, that they took the Mono trail."

Since Swan didn't ask, Jackson didn't bother to mention that Byrnes had the company of Ike Powell along for the ride. "Let's get on their trail, White Beard, it shouldn't take us too long to catch up."

***

Nate Burleson had his hands cuffed in front so he could ride with at least a little comfort, with Byrnes alongside, trailing a mule. Powell rode behind trailing the other mule, as they made their way toward Mono Lake and the road north to Carson City. This route added one day extra to the ride but was easier on both the riders and the animals.

The road was built for wagons, large wagons, so was easy to follow through the high mountains to the east of the Sierra Nevada. There were still large rocks that seemed to grow through every spring, heavy forest lined either side of the trail, and often, at the bottom of a steep passage, mule skinners and riders would find open meadow areas, usually with a spring-fed stream running through. There was enough regular traffic on the road that snow from the recent storms was pretty much beaten down. They twisted and turned, went uphill and down, working their way out of the high country.

"We won't be breaking trail, Powell. It was rough coming up the other side yesterday," Byrnes said.

"This road is well used, Byrnes. We'll be in mud a little later when the sun beats down on it. What the hell was Burleson babbling about when you brought him into the barn? All I could get out of it was something about a big box of gold."

"He was carrying gold when he hightailed it out of the Carson Valley and he offered a pretty hefty bribe to Swan to let him out. He didn't expect to be turned down. Self-centered as the man is, having an offer of gold and a better life turned down is a shock." Byrnes laughed, getting a stream of foul language from Burleson, and some laughter from Ike Powell.

"Anybody besides us and Swan know about that gold?"

"What you thinkin', Ike?"

"Swan ain't clean, Hawkeye. He's about as crooked as many of the sharks in Aurora. We might want to think about our backs. I was in the saloon last night and saw Swan talking with White Beard Morrison, and that ain't good. Morrison robs stage coaches on this very road, and it wouldn't surprise me if Swan helped him some."

"One thing we know, Ike, if they are planning something, they have to be behind us. You've used this trail many times," Byrnes said. "Where would you hit us if you could ride up behind us?"

Ike Powell almost laughed at the question, remembering the various spots on the road where stages had been stopped and looted, where ore wagons had been stopped and robbed. "There's a big flat meadow a couple of miles in front of us that would make it easy for them to ride us down."

"What's on this side of that meadow?"

"Kinda like this, deep forest, narrow trail. Oh, Mr. Byrnes, it would be a perfect place to set up a hijack." Powell laughed. "They would be thinking meadow and we'd be waiting for them before the meadow."

"Yup. Get a hidey-hole and jump them. Or, more fun, let them ride on by, and trail them into the meadow. No, easier to jump them in the forest. Let's put on a little speed, Mr. Powell, and find someplace to hide."

Burleson was furious listening to Byrnes and Powell and knew immediately that Powell was right about Swan. He'd let him know about the gold and remembered saying he had a large box of gold. *That deputy didn't take the bribe, but the bastard is willing to steal it*, Burleson fumed. *I won't let that happen. He won't steal my gold.*

Burleson worked on the problem the whole time Byrnes and Powell rode toward where they would make their play. He finally figured the only way he could get away, and keep his gold, was to help Swan in some way.

"Make him grateful," he murmured, "and then I'll have to kill the bastard. All he had to do was let me out of that jail and he would have had some of the gold." Burleson wanted to scream a mountain full of foul language.

Pines, fir, spruce, even some nice cedar grew thick on both sides of the steep trail, and it took just minutes to find a good spot to jump Swan and White Beard, if they really were being followed. "I'll take Burleson and the two mules on this side of the trail and get them nestled out of sight, and set up my hiding place, and you set up on the other side."

"I would usually go along with anything you said, Byrnes, but what you just said would put us in a position where we might shoot each other. Let's both stay on the same side of the trail. Safer, that way."

"I wasn't plannin' on shootin' anyone, Ike, but you're right. We'll stay on the same side. If we don't hear or see anything in an hour, we'll just go on. I'm sure, if they really are coming, that they won't want to be too far behind us."

***

"Where'd you put the animals and the prisoner?"

"Back behind there, about fifty feet or so," Byrnes said. "Can't see 'em from here. He's got his arms wrapped around a pine tree and the horses and mules are tied off, nice and tight."

Each man had a rifle and handgun and they were tucked in behind some downed trees alongside the trail when they heard approaching horses and men talking. "Let's let 'em get nice and close, Ike." Byrnes could see two men on horses coming down the trail and recognized one of them as Deputy Swan. He just gave a resigned nod to Powell, as if to say, "You were right."

There is no more vile person than a lawman turned criminal, Hawkeye was thinking, watching the two men ride toward him. *He's still got that badge pinned to his coat and probably hasn't given what he's doing a second thought. Well, buster, you're about to get the surprise of your young obnoxious life.*

When the two were within ten yards or so, Byrnes and Powell were about to tell the riders to halt or die when Burleson started yowling about the danger.

"It's a trap," Swan said, trying to get his horse turned on the narrow trail. White Beard Morrison had his revolver out and was shooting into the trees, getting both their horses riled some.

"Stop, both of you. Stop or die," Byrnes shouted, and Morrison took a shot in his direction. It was answered by a rifle shot from Byrnes that knocked White Beard right out of the saddle. Swan was still fighting his horse, trying to pull his revolver, and a heavy chunk of lead ripped through his arm, toppling him to the ground. Swan's weapon fell into the mud.

Byrnes and Powell jumped out from their cover, and ran toward Swan. Powell grabbed the horse by the headstall and Byrnes jerked Swan up to his feet, smashed a hard fist into his face, and followed it with another into his midsection, putting the man out of the fight.

Powell got both horses under control and back in the trees where the other animals were tied off, and slapped Burleson hard across the head. "Dumb damn fool move, mister," he snarled, and slapped him again, harder. "Your stupid squalling just got a man killed," and he smacked him again.

Byrnes brought Swan into the little clearing and dumped him on the ground. "Seems to be bleeding some," Powell said. "Guess I should stop the flow, or just let him bleed out, Mr. Byrnes?"

"Oh, Mr. Powell, sir, I want this man alive when we reach Carson City. Bruised up a bit, bleeding some, but very much alive. I'm pretty sure White Beard Morrison is dead, but I'm going back to check on him. Do your duty as an animal caretaker, Ike." Byrnes laughed, walking back toward the trail and Morrison's body.

They had Morrison's body tied on his horse, and Swan and Burleson, in cuffs, were also firmly attached to their mounts. "If it was summer we'd probably just bury White Beard, but since it's so cold, we'll bring him in. Might be a reward in store for you, Ike. You said he was wanted some."

"Yeah, and posters all say, dead or alive. Glad to be making the ride with you, Hawkeye." He laughed, jabbing Swan, just because he could.

Byrnes led the prisoner's horses and Powell led the mules, and the little train continued on toward Mono Lake and the road north. "These fools didn't bring anything with them, Ike. We'll be on short rations unless we can shoot something today or tomorrow. Might find some deer along the Walker River tomorrow."

"That bullet went right on through Swan's arm, broke the bone on the way, but he won't die on us. He's a whiney little fool, though."

"Men that wear a badge and then dishonor it usually are whiney little cowards, Ike. I might just rip that badge off his shirt and shove it right up his ass if he gives us any trouble. Might do it anyway," he said, with no smile, no little Hawkeye chuckle.

They got down in the valley and made good time going north before it got so dark that they finally had to make camp for the night. Powell gathered firewood while Byrnes took care of the prisoners and the animals, and within a short time they sat around a nice big fire. "Looks like you brought some good side meat, Ike, and some beans, too. I'm hungry."

"I brought side meat and beans for three people for three days, Hawkeye. Now, we are four."

"Well, then, we must divvy this up, all proper like," Byrnes said. You and I will get full rations of side meat and beans, Ike. Swan and Burleson will get half rations of side meat and beans. See? That was easy, eh?"

After supper, Powell redressed Swan's wound and told Hawkeye that there were signs of infection. "I poured a little brandy into the wound, but we're gonna have to keep an eye on it. If he develops a fever, we'll have to take other action."

"You poured good brandy on it? Didn't have any rotgut whiskey?"

Chapter Twenty-One

"It's definitely infected, Hawkeye," Powell said, washing Swan's wound with hot water, and getting ready to redress it. "If the brandy doesn't clean it out today, we'll have to use some gunpowder tonight."

"I've heard about that but never tried it." Hawkeye knelt down to get a good look at the wound. "Right below the elbow, broke bones and ripped up the meat some," he mumbled. "That arm's gonna be useless, Ike. We might as well chop it off now, save all that cleaning and redressing."

Swan howled his shock at the thought of losing his arm, begged Powell not to do it, and Powell could only hold his laughter for a few seconds. "Sumbitch, Hawkeye, he is a crybaby." Ike Powell poured some brandy on the open wound, bringing more screams, and wrapped it tight.

"Just remember, Swan, you wouldn't-a got shot if old Burleson here hadn't done all that yellin' at you. Whack him one, if it'll make you feel better. Alright, Ike, let's get this circus back on the road," and Byrnes jerked Swan to his feet, then Burleson, got White Beard's body tied on his horse, and they rode off toward the north, through mountain passes, along a branch of the Walker River, and just before stopping for the night, Ike spotted a group of antelope off the trail some.

The Sweetwater ranges, rugged, spindly high peaks, almost saw-tooth in looks, are split by the Walker River. The road they were on was originally the Walker trail, laid out by the old mountain-man pioneer. They had passed through deep canyons, across wide meadows and valleys, and seen some of the most beautiful country that California and Nevada shared.

They had moved out of a deep canyon into a wide valley and stumbled on an antelope herd grazing.

Ike Powell didn't say anything, simply raised his rifle, took careful aim, and dropped the animal in one shot. He also caused a wonderful, but short lived, rodeo with Swan getting thrown from his horse, Burleson hanging off to the side of his saddle, and Byrnes cussing like a New York dockworker.

After skinning and cleaning the antelope, and getting supper on the fire, Powell moved to Swan and took off the bloody dressing. "He opened the wound falling off his horse like that. I thought law dogs were good riders, Hawkeye."

"He ain't no law dog, Ike, just a dumb ass criminal. He gonna live?"

"He's lucky it's cold. The infection's bad and there ain't nothing I can do about it except pour some more brandy in the wound. If we leave early in the morning and ride hard, he'll be alive when we reach Carson City."

"Fresh meat," is all Powell said, watching a large chunk of back strap sizzle on an open fire. "We'll make Carson City tomorrow, Hawkeye?"

"At the rate we're moving, we'll be there tomorrow afternoon."

***

"Have you heard anything from Hawkeye Byrnes?" Elmer Barlow asked when Jacob Chance walked into his office that morning.

"No, Barlow, not yet. If he found trouble he would have sent word in some way. Looks like some of these members of the legislature are going to be facing some federal charges as well as what you're offering. The desire for money has some weird ways with some people. Bribery, hypocrisy, lies, and justification are writ large in this little conspiracy, Barlow.

"If Hawkeye finds Burleson, it will be interesting to hear how he'll try to justify every law he broke. I'm sure tired of listening to O'Brien. It's always this way, though," he said, sitting back in one of Barlow's large, leather-covered arm chairs. "The big tough bad guy who everyone fears turns into a crybaby wimp when the cuffs are applied.

"O'Brien was no different than any of the others I've rounded up over the years. Oh, marshal, these cuffs are too tight, oh marshal, it's cold, oh, marshal, don't hit me again," he mimed, trying to hold some laughter in. Barlow was laughing loud as well when Ira Stone walked into the office.

"What's this?" he asked, chewing on a cigar and shaking himself out of a heavy winter coat. "Here are some copies of the federal charges I'm filing later this morning. I'm putting holds on some of your prisoners, Barlow. Let's get 'em tried in federal court, then you can try them in state court."

"We'll let your people feed 'em for a while. That's fine, Stone. We were just wondering when Hawkeye Byrnes would be coming back into town, and whether he would be bringing Burleson in."

"He's got a good head on those shoulders. If anyone can track Burleson down, it would be Byrnes. What are your plans, Chance?"

"Rounding up some more of those that are involved. Burleson and O'Brien managed to get a lot of people involved in this plot of theirs. Spencer was their key, and when he went down it slowed this case way down, but we're getting names from Smith, O'Brien has given a few up, and then the little guys, when we catch them, give it all up." He laughed.

"Keep me advised on Byrnes," Ira Stone said. "Burleson and O'Brien are big on my federal list."

Chance and Barlow talked some more and Chance left to have an early lunch with Jenny and the kids at

Stanfield's big house. Augie Roark would be there, the judge of course, and Jerrod and Elaine Stockton.

***

Byrnes' little caravan topped a ridge late that day, and they could see the vast Carson Valley spread in front of them. "We'll drop out of the Pine Nut range in the morning, and have just about fifty miles to go, Powell. We won't make Carson City today, like I thought, but it won't be a hard ride tomorrow.

"Is your patient going to be with us for the final ride?"

"He's hurtin', the infection is bad, but his fever isn't out of control, so I think we will bring him in alive, Hawkeye. It wouldn't hurt my feeling to kick his ass some, but I won't."

"We'll pass right through Burleson's ranch land tomorrow, Ike. Maybe we can prod him some and he'll give us a talk on what it means to be a well-off rancher." Burleson hurled some more foul language at the two men.

"Do what you can tonight and tomorrow to keep Swan alive, Ike. "I want that bastard to go to prison, and I want his fellow prisoners to know he was a lawman once. I can't think of a better end for him." His anger hadn't let up since he found out that Swan was going to attempt the robbery, and it would have given him great delight to have shot the man dead.

Camp was made in a stand of Piñon pine with good grass for the animals, and good wood for a fire. "At least this time of year we won't be fighting skeeters," Powell said, getting a good fire going. "We'll have to hang the rest of that antelope carcass from one of these trees, Byrnes. There are wolves and bears in this country," he said with just a hint of a wink.

"The bears will rip a camp apart if they smell fresh meat," Byrnes said, looking straight at Swan. "This is bear country, and they can smell blood for miles and miles."

They ate antelope and beans that night, and got started early the next morning with platters of side meat and beans. Swan had to be tied to the saddle as the infection had spread and the fever was running high. "He'll be in bad shape when we reach Carson City, Hawkeye," Powell said as they moved off. "We've got good weather, still. It's almost level all the way in, isn't it?"

"Surely is, Ike. We'll ride on good roads most of the way through the valley, and the road is well maintained. This'll be the easiest fifty miles you've ever made."

They didn't stop anywhere along the road, except for little personal stops, and neared the capital late in the day. They had stopped a rider coming past them and asked that he ride fast and find Marshal Chance and let him know they were close.

A couple of hours later, Chance rode up with a big smile. "I'm glad you made it safe, Hawkeye. What have we got here?" he said, looking over the caravan of horses, mules, bodies, injured, cuffed, and uncuffed.

Hawkeye Byrnes introduced Chance to Ike Powell and spent the next hour telling the story of his visit to Aurora. "We'll get Burleson set up at the state prison and Swan under guard at the hospital, and I think you and Mr. Powell will need to join me and Elmer Barlow in warm drinks and hot food," Chance said.

It was a tired crew that rode into the capital late that afternoon, and of course it took longer than anticipated getting Swan to the hospital and Burleson to the prison, but the three finally rode up to the St. Charles Hotel and found comfortable seats in the opulent saloon.

"Whiskey," was all Byrnes said, flopping down.

Chapter Twenty-Two

It was two weeks of intense work with the attorney general's staff before Chance was able to make plans to bring his family home. "I have a message for you, Chance," Barlow said one morning. "Ira Stone wants to see you in his office at eleven. There aren't enough words to thank you for your service, marshal. My people can take it from here, I think. You're heading back for Preston in the morning?"

"That's the plan, yes sir. It's been a pleasure working for you, General Barlow, but to be blunt about it, you need a full time working law dog as your chief inspector."

"I know I do, Chance, and Stone is helping me line up some candidates. I guess I missed out on grabbing Byrnes. He's going into the U.S. Marshal Service, I hear."

"Yes, he is, and he'll be a good one. Ira is going to be his sponsor, so he'll have good back up from the start." They shook hands and Chance left the office and headed for Ira Stone's office, down Carson Street about a block or two. "I wonder what he has on his mind?" he muttered, trudging through old and grimy snow left over from the last blizzard to make its frenzied way through the capital.

He was ushered into Stone's office immediately and found Hawkeye Byrnes in the office as well. "I thought you might want to be a witness to this little procedure," Stone said, chewing on yet another unlit cigar. "If you would be kind enough to remove that sombrero of yours and stand next to this gentleman, we'll get started."

Chance tried to hide a grand smile and gave up on that, whacked Byrnes across the shoulders and stood next to him. Byrnes was asked to raise his right hand and

Nevada's Federal Attorney, and retired U.S. Marshal Ira Stone, swore the young man in as Deputy United States Marshal, and presented him with a bent and well-worn badge.

"That badge was worn by a dear friend of mine who turned it in about fifteen years ago for a new one. It had got all bent up like that in one hell of a fight we were involved in," Ira Stone said with a smirk and a glance at Chance. "The dent in the middle is from a small caliber pistol shot from too far away, and at a different target, I might add, and the one leg was bent crooked by a gambling table that came sailing through the air.

"That badge carries a lot of history, my friend. Wear it with pride knowing it belonged to Jacob Chance, U.S. marshal."

"I'm speechless," Byrnes said as Stone pinned the badge to his wool vest. "Thank you."

"I wasn't aware you still had that, Ira, and I can't think of anyone more qualified to wear it. Congratulations, marshal," he said, shaking hands with the quivering Byrnes. "For the time being, you'll be working under the direction of Stone, and probably eventually you'll be transferred to other districts. You'll not find a better man to work for and learn from than Ira.

"To change the subject, we're heading back to Preston in the morning. Jenny wants both of you to come to supper tonight. We'll feed the kids early and we'll eat about eight. Okay with you two?"

They nodded their heads yes, everyone shook hands, and Chance headed out the door for one last walk around the city. "With a little luck the only visits from now on will be driving herds to Hank Adams' feed lots." He snickered. He stuck his head inside the Capitol building to see if he could run into Jerrod Stockton and instead ran into that reporter from Virginia City.

"It's been a real pleasure writing stories about you, Marshal Chance," the young Mark Twain said, his moustache dancing some and his eyes, as always, twinkling. "As you pointed out to me, once, a couple of my stories about you were quite factual."

"Indeed they were, Mr. Twain. Any good news coming out of these hallowed halls?"

He laughed. "Nary a peep, sir, and even if there were, I wouldn't report such nonsense. Good day," he said, and marched out of the building. Chance had to chuckle, thinking what a strange man, and what fun it was to read what he wrote. He couldn't find Stockton, and made his way back to Jenny and the children to finish what little packing he had to do for tomorrow's ride home.

***

"There's a nest of thieves settled in near Pioche in eastern Nevada, Hawkeye. They've robbed banks on both sides of the Nevada-Utah border, they've held up numerous stage coaches, and taken bullion from several of the mines in that district." Ira Stone had a handful of papers he was stuffing in a leather pouch.

"Here's all the information I have, names and crimes, and some people out there that might be available to help. Here's your runnin' money, keep careful track of your spending, and put those people out of work."

Deputy U.S. Marshal Hawkeye Byrnes slipped out of Stone's office, that bent and weathered badge pinned tightly in place, and went to his apartment above the hardware store to go over the paperwork and pack for his first official job. "From a little crib in Waco, Texas to deputy U.S. marshal, and I'm just twenty-five," he muttered. "From drunks on C Street in Virginia City to bank robbers in Pioche," and he found himself laughing right out loud, walking down Carson Street.

He rode out of Carson City the next morning well before sunrise for the long trip across the entire state of Nevada. The sky was bright with stars, the wind was a gentle breeze, and the air temperature, this twentieth day of February, hovered near the zero mark. Hawkeye was wrapped in a buffalo robe coat and wore heavy rabbit skin gloves that were wrapped in a blanket of wool. "I refuse to be cold," he said with a snarl that was followed by a wry smile and twinkle in his eyes.

"Pioche," he said, over and over. "The name is certainly strange. I wonder just what it is I'm riding into?"

***

It was a sad supper on the one hand and a warm and friendly supper on the other that night at the Chance table, Ira Stone and his wife, Justice Stanfield and Elaine, and Senator Stockton getting ready to send Chance and family home to Preston. Stanfield provided a standing rib of elk roast that Jenny prepared with potatoes and other vegetables, and finished the meal off with apple pies.

"We won't even have left-overs in the wagon on the way home tomorrow," Jenny said, clearing the table. "We cleaned our plates." She laughed, and Chance brought out some snifters and a bottle of brandy, and the men made their way to the living room.

"The forecast is clear sailing, Chance," Jerrod Stockton said. "Just you and the family? No protection or outriders? Do you think that's smart?"

"Of that whole mess of criminals, everyone is either dead or in prison, Jerrod. This will be a nice mid-winter ride, and we'll be home in two days, unless of course you'd like to ride along with us."

Only chuckles from several answered that challenge, and Stanfield sat as quiet as Chance had ever seen the man. "Amos, is there something bothering you?"

"The only reason I'm alive is because of you, Jacob Chance. The only reason Preston survived is because of you and Ira Stone, and the only reason Preston continues is because of Senator Jerrod Stockton. I'm overwhelmed by it all, Jacob. I'm surrounded by historic figures."

It was very quiet for a minute or less, and Ira Stone broke the reverie. "Bah!" he said. "I'm going home. Jacob, have a good trip home, take care of your family, and I'll be down to visit someday soon." General laughter followed him out the door, and Amos Stanfield stood, shook hands with Stockton and Chance, and left as well.

"I guess I'll gather up Elaine and take off, too, Jacob. Have a good trip home, and tell everyone just how hard I'm working up here," Stockton said, followed by more laughter.

It was very late that night that Jacob and Jenny finally fell into bed. "I'll be so glad to be home and in my own bed," he said, holding her tightly to him.

"It was eight years or so ago, Marshal Chance, that you told me you didn't even have a home, slept on the ground more than in a bed, and couldn't imagine living any other way. Now, listen to you."

"It's all your fault, and I miss my cows." He chuckled, took a light punch to the shoulders, and the two fell asleep.

***

Just as Chance predicted, the trip back to Preston was as uneventful as possible. He drove the wagon into the ranch toward the end of the second day with a wide smile. Little Jake had done most of the driving and Chance had to admonish him more than once for his language. "That's how Cookie taught me how to talk to the horses, Papa," he said.

"I guess I'll have to have a word with Cookie, as well," Chance said, doing his best to hide a crooked smile.

"You have to remember who might be near enough to hear what you're saying, Jake. Your Mama doesn't like that kind of language, and a gentleman would never talk like that in front of a lady."

"Welcome home," Buck Colby said, coming out of the bunkhouse. He helped Jennifer down, grabbed little Missy, and shook hands with the boss. "You missed the party, Chance. That big old Texas cowboy, Slim Crockett, and Clementine Bullis got married yesterday, and Roger threw one fine shindig."

"I'm sorry we missed that," Jennifer said, taking Missy back. "Looks like the ranch is still in one piece."

"You got back just in time," he said, starting to unhitch the team. "Looks like an early spring and a good calf crop. We haven't had to pull a one, yet, and I'll bet this is the largest crop of calves yet."

It took a couple of hours to get the wagon unloaded and the contents sorted. A light supper of cold meats and some pie followed, and Jenny got the children put to bed and collapsed on a sofa next to Chance.

"I don't ever want to leave this ranch again unless I'm driving a herd of fat cows somewhere," she whispered. "I enjoyed being in Carson City, I was only terrified, frightened out of my wits half a dozen times," she said with a chuckle, "and I'm never leaving here again."

"We'll get up early tomorrow, Jenny, and ride through the herds. I love watching those young calves running and jumping, and I'll bet we'll find some mighty pregnant mares out there, too."

"I meant to tell you before we left Carson City. We're pregnant again, Marshal Chance. Should be here in time for the fall roundup, again. Do you plan these things?" She got a warm pat on her cute little bottom, felt the big man snuggle close, and heard a comfortable snore in her ear within minutes.

About Johnny Gunn

Writing news copy for print and broadcast was an education in deadline writing, something that has carried into my fiction writing. I put demands on myself as far as writing time is concerned, and refuse to accept the idea of writer's block. Just try to tell your editor you can't do the article on the little girl's murder because you are suffering from writer's block. My wife, Patty, and I live north of Reno on a small hobby farm.

Social Media Links:

Member, Western Fictioneers

Member, International Thriller Writers

Facebook: https://www.facebook.com/johnny.gunn.31

Blog: http://johnny-gunn.blogspot.com/

Twitter: https://twitter.com/johnnygunn11

If you enjoyed this story, check out these other Solstice Publishing books by Johnny Gunn:

Jacob Chance Novels

Jacob Chance U.S. Marshall

Land law, water rights, deeds of ownership? Boring. Unless of course, people are shooting at you because of them. The Civil War has disrupted thousands of lives, including that of Sarah Jackson, whose husband was killed for not joining the Confederate Army in Georgia. Sarah and her daughter flee to Nevada Territory and are eligible for homestead rights. After claiming her one hundred sixty acres in the lush Golden Valley, her world crumbles again.

http://bookgoodies.com/a/B00XWBQ0OO

A Good Life Cut Short

Jacob Chance, U.S. Marshal just made the biggest move of his life. He retired from the Marshal Service and planned to move to a ranch in Nevada Territory, marry a beautiful young woman, and not spend the rest of his life chasing criminals, lunatics, and murderers. Lives are lost, lives are endangered, and a new way of life is threatened. Can Jacob Chance really retire?

http://bookgoodies.com/a/B01F29L6ZQ

Novels

Paradise Challenged

Thornton Holiday is a murderer and a bank robber. He's a man with a plan—a plan to create an outlaw haven in the New Mexico community of Plainsville. The village is overrun with the meanest outlaws in the west and fights back with the help of a fourteen-year-old boy who demands to be considered a man.

http://bookgoodies.com/a/B015QFSMAS

So Young So Dead

The vicious murder of a young girl leads to the disintegration of the Sandesta County Sheriff's Department. A homophobic district attorney, a misogynist sergeant of detectives, and a serial killer all come together in So Young, So Dead. Many issues facing law enforcement today are as much social issues as they are criminal. They have all found a home in Sandesta County.

http://bookgoodies.com/a/B0193RHXXW

A Good Life Cut Short

Jacob Chance, U.S. Marshal just made the biggest move of his life. He retired from the Marshal Service and planned to move to a ranch in Nevada Territory, marry a beautiful young woman, and not spend the rest of his life chasing criminals, lunatics, and murderers.

His soon-to-be brother in law, Jim Stokes, already on probation for attacking the marshal, goes on a murderous killing rampage and forces Chance to once again wear the badge. Another man, this one mad with gold fever threatens the town of Preston, Nevada while Chance chases young Stokes across the Silver State.

Lives are lost, lives are endangered, and a new way of life is threatened. Can Jacob Chance really retire?

http://bookgoodies.com/a/B01F29L6ZQ

To Serve and Deceive

Jason Caldwell, retired Hollywood producer and screenwriter, looked forward to years of fishing the oceans of the world. Instead, he married a gorgeous college professor who was also an undercover FBI agent. Jason didn't discover that little aspect of her life until after she was blown away by international gangsters. There are battles on the high seas, battles in the redwood forests, and battles in Washington, DC.

http://bookgoodies.com/a/B01LOBFVDE

Short Stories

Miss Minerva's Sheriff

She was tall and thin, had a .45 strapped on, and said she wanted to make him the happiest man in the world. The sheriff had a reputation that said he was tough, fair, and could shoot straight, but could he stand up to Miss Minerva? And what will the town think? A quirky western romance, Miss Minerva's Sheriff is set in the little Nevada community of Ione, once the Nye County Seat, during the worst mid-winter blizzard ever. He saved her once, now it's her turn.

http://bookgoodies.com/a/B01CEUMZTW

Red Light Raven

The IRS agent was a pit-bull of an investigator and when county officials started turning up dead, he found himself in more of an investigation than just picking off errant taxpayers. There was a definite conspiracy involved in the deaths, but the county officials were also involved in criminal activity surrounding a brothel named The Raven's Nest. A madman was out to clean up the county, and he didn't care how many had to die to accomplish that.

http://bookgoodies.com/a/B01G2B7RUG

Over There

Has Hector Wellington gone mad, or are there other forces at work? Are these evil forces at work? He asks, "Who am I and why am I here?" and he gets a gut wrenching answer after a terrifying experience.

http://bookgoodies.com/a/B01M4QXY6U

Slick's Special Christmas

Blizzards, wild cows with long horns, and singing buckaroos. It's Slick's Special Christmas.

http://bookgoodies.com/a/B01N1OYVPT

Anthologies

Adventures in Love

From a western gal in pursuit of the local sheriff to a single mom running a cooking show with her small children, romance blossoms in many situations. These wonderful stories prove that love is for all ages.

A.A. Schenna, Alex Pilalis, Donna Alice Patton, EB Sullivan, Heidi Renee Mason, Johnny Gunn, Susan Lynn Solomon, Mark Newhouse, and Susanne Matthews delight romantics on this special holiday with their tales of love.

http://bookgoodies.com/a/B01BH2F7E8

Now I Lay Me Down To Sleep Vol 4

Sleep is impossible after reading these eight tales of things that go bump in the night…

Mysterious Warrior Battles Evil Coven…

Haunted wedding dress horror story…

Every secret has a cost…

Who am I and why am I here?

Long hidden secrets emerge from the pond…

Unexpected consequences from an interruption…

Don't plan on the usual housewarming!

The perfect relationship from hell!

Sadie K. Frazier, Josie Montano, S.C. Alban, Johnny Gunn, K.C. Sprayberry, Debbie De Louise, Archimede Fusillo, and Alex Pilalis present eight stories of horror sure to have you screaming!

http://bookgoodies.com/a/B01M7URA5Z

A Winter Holiday 2016

A season for joy…

A season for celebration…

A season for family…

Solstice Publishing presents eleven talented authors with a dozen stories that portray the winter holiday season in many ways. Each tale will fill you with wonder, joy, and a sense of carned togetherness.

Celebrate with K.C. Sprayberry, Donna Alice Patton, Johnny Gunn, Susan Lynn Solomon, Debbie De Louise, Elle Marlow, Leah Hamrick, Eden S. Clark, E.B. Sullivan, M.A. Cortez, and Rebecca L. Frencl this winter holiday season.

http://bookgoodies.com/a/B01N41UOYH

www.ingramcontent.com/pod-product-compliance
Lightning Source LLC
Chambersburg PA
CBHW051135020726
47501CB00005B/1512